NUCLEAR
JELLYFISH
OF
NEW
JERSEY

"Your books give me the chills! I really, really love them, but I don't know what one I like best."

-Jeff M., age 12, Utah

"I was read WISCONSIN WEREWOLVES, and now I'm freaked out, because I live in Wisconsin. I never knew we had werewolves."

-Angie T., age 9, Wisconsin

"I have every single AMERICAN CHILLER except VIRTUAL VAMPIRES OF VERMONT. I love all of them!"

-Cole H ., age 11, Michigan

"The lady at the bookstore told me I should read NEBRASKA NIGHTCRAWLERS, so I did. I just finished it, and it was GREAT!"

-Stephen S., age 8, Oklahoma

"SOUTH CAROLINA SEA CREATURES is the best book in the whole world!"

-Ashlee L, age 11, Georgia

"I read your books every night!"

-Aaron. W, age 10, New York

"I love your books! When I read AMERICAN CHILLERS, it's like I'm part of the story!"

-Leroy N., age 8, Rhode Island

"KREEPY KLOWNS OF KALAMAZOO is my favorite. It was awesome! I did a book report about it, and I got an 'A'!

-Samantha T., age 10, Illinois

Don't miss these exciting, action-packed books by Johnathan Rand:

Michigan Chillers:

#1: Mayhem on Mackinac Island
#2: Terror Stalks Traverse City
#3: Poltergeists of Petoskey
#4: Aliens Attack Alpena
#5: Gargoyles of Gaylord
#6: Strange Spirits of St. Ignace
#7: Kreepy Klowns of Kalamazoo
#8: Dinosaurs Destroy Detroit
#9: Sinister Spiders of Saginaw
#10: Mackinaw City Mummies
#11: Great Lakes Ghost Ship
#12: AuSable Alligators
#13: Gruesome Ghouls of Grand Rapids
#14: Bionic Bats of Bay City

American Chillers:

#1: The Michigan Mega-Monsters
#2: Ogres of Ohio
#3: Florida Fog Phantoms
#4: New York Ninjas
#5: Terrible Tractors of Texas
#6: Invisible Iguanas of Illinois
#7: Wisconsin Werewolves
#8: Minnesota Mall Mannequins
#9: Iron Insects Invade Indiana
#10: Missouri Madhouse
#11: Poisonous Pythons Paralyze Pennsylvania
#12: Dangerous Dolls of Delaware
#13: Virtual Vampires of Vermont
#14: Creepy Condors of California
#15: Nebraska Nightcrawlers
#16: Alien Androids Assault Arizona
#17: South Carolina Sea Creatures
#18: Washington Wax Museum
#19: North Dakota Night Dragons
#20: Mutant Mammoths of Montana
#21: Terrifying Toys of Tennessee
#22: Nuclear Jellyfish of New Jersey
#23: Wicked Velociraptors of West Virginia

Freddie Fernortner, Fearless First Grader:

#1: The Fantastic Flying Bicycle
#2: The Super-Scary Night Thingy
#3: A Haunting We Will Go
#4: Freddie's Dog Walking Service
#5: The Big Box Fort
#6: Mr. Chewy's Big Adventure
#7: The Magical Wading Pool

Adventure Club series:

#1: Ghost in the Graveyard
#2: Ghost in the Grand
#3: The Haunted Schoolhouse

For Teens:

PANDEMIA: A novel of the bird flu and the end of the world
(written with Christopher Knight)

AMERICAN CHILLERS

America's #1 Series for MAXIMUM Chills!

#22: Nuclear Jellyfish of New Jersey

Johnathan Rand

An AudioCraft Publishing, Inc. book

This book is a work of fiction. Names, places, characters and incidents are used fictitiously, or are products of the author's very active imagination.

Book storage and warehouses provided by Chillermania!©
Indian River, Michigan

Warehouse security provided by:
Lily Munster and Scooby-Boo

American Chillers #22: Nuclear Jellyfish of New Jersey
ISBN 13-digit: 978-1-893699-93-9

Librarians/Media Specialists:
PCIP/MARC records available at www.americanchillers.com

Cover illustration by Dwayne Harris
Cover layout and design by Sue Harring

Printed in USA

NUCLEAR
JELLYFISH
OF
NEW
JERSEY

VISIT CHILLERMANIA!

WORLD HEADQUARTERS FOR BOOKS BY JOHNATHAN RAND!

Yooperland

Indian River

Alpena

Traverse City

MICHIGAN

CHILLERMANIA!

*I-75 Exit 313
then south
1 mile!*

Mt. Pleasant

Bay City

Grand Rapids

Lansing

Detroit

Kalamazoo

Visit the HOME for books by Johnathan Rand! Featuring books, hats, shirts, bookmarks and other cool stuff not available anywhere else in the world! Plus, watch the American Chillers website for news of special events and signings at *CHILLERMANIA!* with author Johnathan Rand! Located in northern lower Michigan, on I-75! Take exit 313 . . . then south 1 mile! For more info, call (231) 238-0338. And be afraid! Be veeeery afraaaaaaiiiid . . . .

At first, I didn't like New Jersey. Oh, there's nothing wrong with the state at all, and now I love it here. But my family moved here from Tennessee, and I had to leave all my friends behind. That was really, really hard.

My name is Shayleen Mills, and I live in Medford, New Jersey. We moved here last summer, when my dad took a job here. I didn't want to leave Tennessee, but soon, I made a bunch of new friends.

And now I like New Jersey. It's a lot different from Tennessee. I can't say I like one state better than the other. It's hard to compare the two, because there are so many cool things about both states.

I can say, however, there is one thing I don't like about Tennessee: toys and toy stores. Earlier this summer, my friends Eric Carter and Mark Bruder had a really freaky thing happen to us, and it had to do with toys that came to life. It was really scary . . . but that's another story altogether.

And, if you want to know the truth, there's something I don't like about New Jersey:

The ocean.

Now, I know what you're probably thinking. You're thinking I can't swim, or I don't like salt water. You're thinking maybe I don't like the hot sun or the sandy beaches. Wrong. I love it all.

It's what's *in* the ocean that I don't like, and I'm not talking about sharks or barracuda or killer whales. I'm talking about something totally different . . . something no one even knew existed, until this summer.

Jellyfish.

Now, jellyfish alone can be bad enough. The sting of a jellyfish can be very painful. Sometimes,

it can be fatal.

But, I'm not talking about plain old jellyfish. I'm talking about radioactive creatures—nuclear jellyfish—that are far, far more dangerous than normal jellyfish. And if I thought my ordeal with terrifying toys was bad, it couldn't compare with the horrors my family and friends went through in a small vacation town on the east coast of New Jersey.

We moved from Murfreesboro, Tennessee, to Medford, New Jersey, in the middle of summer. It took us a few days to get settled in to our new home, because we had a lot of things to unpack. In fact, for a few days, the only things I had in my bedroom were my bed, a chair, and a few boxes of clothing.

But we finally got everything unpacked and put away, and I arranged everything in my room just like it had been at our old home in Tennessee. I have a little brother named Lee, and I helped him arrange his room. Actually, I was the only one who did the arranging. He just played around, mostly. Lee is only two years old, but he manages to get into all sorts of trouble. He's really curious, and he's always poking around where he shouldn't be. We have to keep an eye on him all the time, so he doesn't do something to hurt himself. Sure, he doesn't *mean* to get into trouble . . . but he's only two and he doesn't know any better.

I, however, am a lot older, and I *should* know better. Usually, I can spot trouble coming a mile away. In fact, I knew there was something strange about that toy store in Tennessee. And I knew the toys meant trouble.

But how was I to know about the trouble that was coming when we went on a weekend vacation to the New Jersey coast? How was I supposed to know the four days we spent in Wildwood, a popular tourist destination in southeastern New Jersey, would be a disaster?

We had only been in our new home in Medford for about a month when Dad suggested we take a short vacation. He'd been working long days at his new job. He said he had to, because

there were a lot of new things to learn. But he said he needed a break and decided we should take a short vacation. Not just a vacation, but a trip to the Atlantic Ocean!

That would be awesome! I hadn't been anywhere else in New Jersey except Medford. In fact, I've never even seen the ocean! I couldn't wait to wade and swim and splash in the waves and feel the hot sand between my toes. I couldn't wait to hear the roar of the surf and seagulls crying out overhead.

Mom, Lee, and I went shopping the day before we left. We bought some new towels and a big beach umbrella, and I got a new bathing suit. Mom also bought Lee a plastic pail and a few plastic shovels, so he could play in the sand.

And the next morning when we drove to Wildwood, I couldn't believe it! It had the coolest amusement park I'd ever seen in my life! Dad had told me all about it, but I never imagined it would be so big. We drove by a place called the Boardwalk, where I saw a huge, twisting roller coaster; a gigantic Ferris wheel; and lots more rides. There were gobs and gobs of people all over the place! The sun was shining, the surf was pounding, and there were lots of people swimming.

"This is incredible!" I said, nearly shouting from the back seat of the car.

"I thought you'd like it," Dad said. "And the weather is supposed to be hot and sunny the whole time we're here. After we check into our hotel, we'll relax on the beach for a while before we go sightseeing. I think we're all going to have a great time."

Now, my dad is almost always right about *everything*. He's one of the smartest dads in the world, in my opinion.

But this time, he was wrong. Sure, we all started out having a great time, but it wasn't long before things went very wrong . . . only moments after I'd waded into the ocean.

We found our hotel, which faced the beach. It was so cool! We were on the second floor, and there was a sliding glass door and a deck right off our room. There was a small table and a few chairs on the deck, in case we wanted to eat outside or just relax. Mom slid open the glass panel door, and the room was suddenly awash with warm ocean air. Below, on the beach, there were people everywhere! Colorful beach towels and umbrellas dotted the white sand. People walked along the shore and swam in the water. Several people were trying to surf, but it didn't look like the waves were big enough.

"Rides! Rides!" Lee squealed as he looked at the amusement park in the distance. He was excited, too, but he wasn't big enough to go on most of the rides. Still, I knew he would have a lot of fun.

"Let's get unpacked so we can go the beach!" I said, turning and walking back into the hotel room. Mom and Lee followed.

"I'll bet we'll see some beautiful sunrises," Dad said as we unpacked our clothes and put them in the dresser.

"*You* will," Mom smirked. "We're on vacation. I'm planning on sleeping late."

We changed into our swimsuits, and it wasn't very long before we were ready to go. Mom packed a beach bag with towels, some bottled water, snacks, and Lee's plastic pail and shovels. She handed me a bottle of sun screen.

"Shayleen, can you put some sun screen on your brother?" she asked.

"Sure," I said.

"And make sure you get enough for

yourself."

"Gotcha," I replied. "Lee . . . come here."

Lee was standing by the open sliding glass door, watching the sky and the waves and the people. When I called him, he walked over to me.

"I've got to put this sun screen on you, okay?" I said. "Don't make a fuss like last time."

Before we'd moved, Mom and Lee and I went to the beach. Mom asked me to put sun screen on Lee, but he was so freaked out that he ran away! I didn't know what his problem was. It was just sun screen. I had to chase him all over the beach, catch him, and take him back to the picnic area. He even started crying!

Lee shook his head as I opened the bottle. "No, no, no," he said.

And that's when Mom stepped in. "Lee," she said sternly, "if you don't let your sister put sun screen on you, you're staying in the hotel room."

Lee looked at Mom, and I could tell he got the message. He didn't fuss a bit as I rubbed sun screen all over him.

"There," I said. "All done."

After I covered my exposed skin with sun

screen, I handed the bottle back to Mom. Dad had gone to get a bucket of ice, and he returned.

"You guys all set?" he asked.

"Yeah!" I said. "Let's go to the beach!"

"Beach! Beach! Beach!" Lee exclaimed. He bounced up and down like a kangaroo.

We took the stairs down and came out on the beach. Again, I was hit by warm, salty air. The sand was hot beneath my feet, but I didn't mind.

And we get to spend four whole days here! I thought. *What fun!*

We found a place on the beach, and Mom and Dad spread out a blanket. Dad opened up the umbrella. It was huge! He positioned it so we could sit in its shade, out of the burning rays of the sun.

But I wasn't sitting around! I wanted to be in the water!

"Let's go swimming!" I said.

"I'll take you and Lee down to the shore," Dad said.

"I'm going to stay right here and read," Mom said, and she reached into her bag and pulled out a book. "You guys have fun."

Dad, Lee, and I held hands as we walked toward the ocean, skirting around dozens of people sitting or lying on blankets. Some kids were playing catch with a football, and I saw a few kites in the air. Seagulls whirled above, gracefully gliding on currents of air.

When we reached the water, I let go of Dad's hand.

"Remember what I told you," he said. "Don't go in farther than your waist. The ocean is very different than the lakes and pools you've been in. The currents here can be really strong. We don't want you pulled out to sea and eaten by a killer whale."

"Dad," I said, rolling my eyes. *Killer whales,* I thought. *Right.*

He laughed and sat down in the sand. Lee was carrying his pail and a blue plastic shovel, and he knelt down and started to dig. Just what he was digging for, I didn't know. But it looked like he was having fun.

I waded into the water. The surf came in and splashed up to my knees. The water was cool and refreshing. Then, it reversed and receded back. I was standing in ankle-deep water.

I continued walking out into the water. There were people all around, talking, laughing, splashing, and playing. Everyone was having just as much fun as I was!

But there was also something else around.

Something I'd only seen on television and movies.

A shark.

It was coming right at me, but by the time I saw the dorsal fin emerge from the water, it was only a few feet away . . . and there was no way I could escape.

I shrieked, and everyone around me stopped what they were doing. I could see the dark form of the shark, and before I could even move, he—

hit my leg and bounced off?!?!

I heard a boy laughing nearby, and I turned. Dad was standing at the shoreline a few dozen yards away. He'd heard my panicky shriek and was looking at me, worried.

I looked down. The shark swam to the right of me, but, by now, I'd realized it wasn't a *real* shark. It was a *toy*. A remote-controlled machine.

More toys, I thought, recalling my recent experience in Tennessee.

I waved to Dad to let him know I was okay. Then, I looked down at the shark in the water. Now that it was close, I could easily see it wasn't real. There was a large propeller behind his tail, and the fin moved from left to right. I figured that was how the shark turned.

But he had to be controlled by someone, and, at that very moment, a boy about my age sloshed up to me. He had thick, black hair, and he was very tan.

"Gotcha good, huh?" he said with a wide grin.

"That wasn't very nice," I said. "I was really scared. Only for a minute, though."

"I bought him at the electronics store at the mall," the boy said. "Up close, he doesn't look real. But people see his fin coming at them, and they freak out. I scared a little old lady this morning. She flipped her lid!"

"That's not very nice," I repeated. Secretly, though, I thought a remote-controlled shark would be fun to have. It might be fun to scare people, as long as no one got hurt.

"Hey, I'm just having fun," the boy said. "I'm sorry if you got freaked out."

He reached down and pulled the remote-controlled shark from the water. It was big—nearly three feet long—but the boy carried it easily, so I figured it must not be very heavy.

"What's your name?" the boy asked.

"Shayleen Mills," I replied. "What's yours?"

"Tony," he replied, and he dropped the shark into the water. "Actually, it's Antonio. But everyone calls me Tony. Where are you from?"

"Medford," I replied. "Actually, I'm from Tennessee. We moved to Medford last month, and we came here for a short vacation."

"How do you like it so far?" Tony asked. He was fiddling with the remote control box in his hand, and the shark was swimming circles around us.

"Oh, everything was going great," I replied, "until I was attacked by a shark."

He looked up at me and smiled. I was only kidding, and he knew it.

"Well, if you're here on vacation, you have

to visit my family's water park. We own it."

"You . . . you *own* a water park?" I said in disbelief.

"Not *me,* silly," Tony said. "My Dad. My Dad and his brother, actually. It's right over there." He pointed toward the amusement park in the distance. "It's pretty cool. You should check it out while you're here. I can get you in free, if you want."

"Really?!?!" I exclaimed. "That would be awesome! I've never been to a water park before."

"There aren't any water parks in Tennessee?" Tony asked.

"Oh, Tennessee has water parks," I replied. "But I've never been to one."

"Come on," Tony said. "I'll take you there."

"I've got to check with my dad, first," I said. I pointed. "He's right over there."

We waded through the surf to the shore, where Dad was helping Lee build a sand castle. I introduced Dad to Tony.

"Tony's Dad owns a water park," I said. "It's right over there. Can I go see it?"

Dad looked at his watch. "Yes, but be back

at our hotel room by five. We're going to go out for dinner."

Cool!

Tony tucked his remote controlled shark under his arm, and we started walking along the shoreline, weaving in and around dozens of people. The sand at my feet was peppered with all sorts of shells, some seaweed, and a few stones.

"Watch it!" Tony suddenly exclaimed as he made a quick sidestep and looked down. His voice was so filled with alarm that I stopped walking and stared down at an object in the sand.

"Eeeww," I said. "What's that?"

In the sand by our feet was a blue-green blob. It looked like it could be a partially-inflated plastic bag, but it had long, thin, wisping tentacles—about a dozen of them—splayed all around like hair.

"That's a jellyfish," he said. "Each one of those tentacles has a stinger. If you get stung, you can get really sick . . . or worse."

I'd heard of jellyfish before, but I'd certainly never seen any.

"They live in the water," Tony explained,

"but they wash up on shore all the time. If you see one in the water, stay away from it."

"You don't have to tell me twice," I said. "That thing is *ugly*."

"I think they're cool-looking," Tony said.

That figures. Most boys I know think gross things are cool.

"If I see any, I'll stay away," I said.

"Don't worry too much about them," Tony said. "They can't chase you or anything. Jellyfish don't actually swim."

Of course, *normal* jellyfish wouldn't chase you. *Normal* jellyfish would just drift in the water, waiting for fish or other things to swim by, so they could eat them.

But the jellyfish we would soon encounter weren't *normal*—they were nasty. They were nasty, and they were nuclear.

That's right—nuclear.

And they were about to turn our vacation into a trip of madness.

The water park was a blast! There were slides and rivers and wake pools . . . all kinds of things. People were everywhere, laughing and smiling. Everyone seemed to be having a great time.

And Tony was a lot of fun. He knew a lot of people, and I thought about how lucky he was to be able to live in Wildwood. Think about it: he could live at the water park all summer, and it wouldn't cost him a nickel! Plus, he had the whole beach to play on. I sure wouldn't mind living here all summer.

Later, I went back to the hotel and got ready for dinner. We went to a seafood place with really good food. Lee didn't think so, though. He ate some sort of seafood and wound up barfing on the floor.

When we got back to the hotel, the sun was beginning to set. Our hotel room faced east, so we couldn't see the sunset . . . but what we *could* see was just as good: the amusement park. Neon lights glowed brightly. As it grew darker, the lights seemed to grow brighter, illuminating the rides. It was an incredible sight. Again, I thought about how lucky Tony was to live in Wildwood. He got to experience all of this every single day!   And we only had three days left before we had to leave. Right then, I planned on making the most of my time. I wasn't going to sit in the hotel room any longer than I had to. I wanted to be outside, seeing things, doing things.

Dad sat in a chair, reading a magazine about the area, and Mom was helping Lee into his pajamas.

"Can we go to the amusement park tonight, Mom?" I asked.

Mom shook her head. "Not tonight, Shayleen," she said. "It's getting late."

I looked at the clock on the dresser. "But it's only eight-thirty," I protested.

"We've had a long day already," Mom said. "Let's get some rest, and we'll go to the amusement park and walk the Boardwalk tomorrow."

Then, I had another thought.

"Well, if we're not going to the amusement park tonight, can I go down to the beach to look for seashells?"

Mom thought for a moment. "I guess you could for a little while," she said. "As long as you don't go too far."

"Me go! Me go!" Lee shouted.

"It's past your bedtime already, Mister," Mom said. "And you've already got your pajamas on."

Lee looked disappointed, but he didn't put up a fuss.

"I won't be gone long," I said.

"Take a key so you don't get locked out of the hotel," Dad said. "And there's a flashlight on the counter. Take that, too."

I picked up a key—actually, it was a white plastic card with the name of the hotel printed on it—and shoved it into my front pocket. Then, I snapped up the flashlight. "Back in a while," I said.

"Have fun," Mom said as the door closed behind me.

I hurried down the hall and down the stairs. Outside, the night air was warm and dry. The sky was clear, and I could hear the gentle surf washing the shore. Although the sun hadn't fully set, it was getting dark quickly. Stars twinkled above. The amusement park glowed like some giant alien spacecraft. I could hear the din of distant laughter and shrieks of delight from people enjoying the rides, and I couldn't wait until I had my chance.

Down by the beach, I could see the silhouettes of people as they walked along the shore. Some people were holding hands, others were just walking along. A few kids chased each other. Somewhere, a dog barked.

I walked through the sand in my sneakers. It would have been nice to go barefoot, but I was wary about stepping on something sharp. I wanted to be able to see where I was walking.

At the shore, the crashing waves were loud, and they drowned out the sounds coming from the amusement park. More stars came out as the sun faded, and the crashing surf glowed like a creamy white bar as it rolled into the shore.

I turned on the flashlight and aimed the beam at the sand.

Something moved.

A jellyfish? I wondered.

I swept the beam of light around. Suddenly, it lit up something with glowing eyes and claws, and before I could react, it attacked me!

I jumped back, not sure what the creature was. It wasn't very big—maybe two inches in diameter—but it was *fast*. It moved with surprising speed. It was a yellowish color, with big, shiny black eyes and a single, large claw.

Then, I realized what I was seeing.

A crab, I thought, and I moved closer. I'd never seen a live crab before, but I knew it couldn't hurt me. Unless, of course, I tried to pick him up. If his claw got hold of my finger, I was sure it would hurt a lot.

The crab spun and vanished with soft clacking noises. I tried to find him again, but he was gone. Soon, however, I found another one. It was a green-blue color, and it was a little smaller than the other crab. It, too, moved away with amazing speed.

I could spend days here just learning about the creatures and critters, I thought. *I'll bet New Jersey has all sorts of animals that Tennessee doesn't.*

"What 'cha looking at?" a familiar voice said. I turned and shined the flashlight up. Tony's face appeared, and he covered his eyes with his arm. "Hey, don't blind me."

I lowered the light. "Sorry," I said.

"What are you looking for?" Tony asked, stepping closer.

"Nothing in particular," I said. "But I found some crabs! They were right by my feet!"

"Probably ghost crabs," Tony said. "They're all over the place. You've got to be careful. They'll kill you if they get the chance."

"Really?" I said, shocked.

Tony laughed. "Nope. Just kidding. They don't get very big, but they can move really fast.

They're harmless, just like my remote-controlled shark."

A distant voice—a girl—pierced over the crashing surf.

"Tony! Where are you?!?!"

"Over here!" Tony called back.

"Where?!?!"

"Right here!"

The dark form of a girl appeared not far away. She approached us, and the glow of the flashlight illuminated her features. She was a little shorter than me with straight, dark hair and dark eyes.

"I've been looking all over for you," she said to Tony.

"I've been trying to hide from you," Tony snickered. He looked at me and nodded toward the girl. "Meet my sister, Isobel."

"Hi," I said. "I'm Shayleen."

"That's a pretty name," Isobel said.

"Thanks," I replied.

Isobel turned to Tony. "Mom says you have to be home in fifteen minutes. Uncle Joe and Aunt Kate are coming by for a visit.

"Oh, *that* sounds like fun," Tony said, shaking his head.

"Hey," Isobel said, "it's better than—"

Isobel stopped speaking. Her eyes grew wide, and her arm suddenly shot up, pointing out to sea. *"What is that?!?!"* she said.

Tony and I turned—and stared. There was no explanation for what we were seeing far out in the ocean . . . .

Now, I know this is going to sound really weird, but what we were seeing was a spacecraft of some sort. It *had* to be. It was shaped like an upside-down bowl and it was glowing, changing colors from yellow to blue, then red, then green.

"What in the world *is* that thing?!?!" I asked. "A helicopter of some sort?" Although I already knew it couldn't be a helicopter or a plane or anything like that, I simply refused to believe it was a spaceship.

"I . . . I don't know," Tony stammered. He

sounded scared, too. "It looks like a UFO!"

"UFOs aren't real," I said. "They're just in movies. Have you ever seen anything like this before?"

"Not me," Isobel said.

"Me neither," Tony replied.

While we watched, the strange craft in the distance continued to change colors.

Suddenly, a beam of white light shot out from beneath it, causing a bright reflection on the water below. We could hear a strange humming sound over the crashing waves.

"What's it doing?" Isobel asked. Her voice cracked. She, too, sounded frightened.

"I don't know," Tony said. "But this is too freaky. We've got to tell someone."

I turned my gaze away from the strange craft hovering over the water far out to sea. Not far away, I could see the silhouettes of other people standing and staring. They, too, were seeing the same thing we were seeing. I could even hear some of them gasping and talking.

I looked back out over the ocean. The beam of light retracted, and only the strange, colorful flying saucer remained.

Without warning, it shot up, bursting skyward. Colors blended and faded as the thing rose higher and higher, farther and farther, until it was only a tiny speck. It became smaller and smaller. Then, it vanished.

"I can't believe we just saw that," Isobel said in a voice so low I barely heard her.

"Let's go tell Mom and Dad!" Tony said excitedly. "They're not going to believe it! See you tomorrow, Shayleen! Come to the water park! We'll be there!"

"See you tomorrow," I said, but before I had finished, Tony and Isobel had jogged away.

I looked back out to sea.

I looked up.

Did we really see that? I wondered. *Did we really see an alien spacecraft?*

I'd heard about reported sightings of alien crafts before. In fact, I'd heard about some strange things in Arizona, about how alien androids were supposed to have taken over the Grand Canyon. I'd heard about a place called Roswell, where, years ago, some people believe an alien spaceship crashed. Somewhere, the government was supposed to be hiding the remains of the craft and alien beings. Dad said it was all just a hoax. He said he didn't believe it.

Still, many people have witnessed what they thought were spaceships . . . and now I was one of them. Tony, Isobel, and I had seen *something* that was truly out of this world.

What?

I had no idea. I wasn't sure what we saw, but I knew we'd seen *something*. Others, as it turned out, saw the same thing we did. They saw the colorful, hovering craft. They saw the beam of light shoot down and hit the water.

No one, however, knew what the spaceship had done. Tony, Isobel, and I would know soon enough . . . but by then, it would already be too late.

Just as I had suspected, Mom and Dad didn't believe a word of what I told them. Oh, they were sure I saw *something* . . . but Dad said it must have been a helicopter.

"It wasn't a helicopter!" I said. "It was too bright! It was too fast, and it went up into the sky and disappeared into outer space!"

Dad smiled and shook his head. "It probably just vanished behind the clouds," he said.

"There's not a cloud in the sky!" I insisted, pointing to the sliding glass door that led to the balcony of our hotel room. "Go look."

"Shayleen," Mom said, "I'm sure you saw *something* . . . but it wasn't a flying saucer."

So, I gave up and went to bed. We had two bedrooms in our hotel room . . . but I had to sleep next to my brother in a double bed. Which was fine, as long as he didn't accidentally kick me in the middle of the night.

And, after Mom and Dad went to bed, after all the lights were off, I stayed awake for a long time, wondering what we had seen far out to sea.

It had to be some sort of alien space craft, I thought. *It had to be. Helicopters can't go that fast, and they don't go into space. And planes can't hover in a single spot.*

It was ten fifty-seven according to the glowing green numbers of the clock on the night stand. I couldn't get to sleep, so I got up and walked to the window. In the distance, I could still see the bright lights of the amusement park. I wasn't sure how long it was open, but there seemed to be quite a few people still out and about at this late hour.

I turned and looked in the direction where

we'd spotted the strange, colorful object. I was hoping I would see it again, but, of course, I didn't. The only thing I could see was the reflection of the moon on the ocean and diamond-sharp stars twinkling.

After a few moments, I crawled back into bed. Lee stirred beside me and rolled over on his side.

A flying saucer, I thought. *All this time, I thought anyone who'd claimed to see one was crazy.*

Then, I had another thought.

Maybe I'm the crazy one. Maybe—

No. Tony and Isobel saw the spacecraft, too. There were a lot of people on the Boardwalk and the beach; others must've seen it.

Finally, I fell asleep.

The rising sun woke me early. Blades of sunlight threaded through the window, causing the room to glow orange, pink, and yellow. It looked cool.

Lee was still sleeping, clutching his blue teddy bear. I had forgotten he'd brought it; Lee never sleeps without it.

The door to our room was partially open,

and I could hear the television.

Then, I heard a gasp.

"Oh, my goodness!" I heard Mom say. Then: *"Shayleen! Wake up! Come here, quick!"*

I flew out of bed. Mom sounded frantic, and I
hadn't a clue what was wrong.

"*Shayleen!*" she called again.

"Coming!" I said as I came through the door.
"What's going on?"

Mom and Dad were seated on the couch.
The sliding glass door was open, and warm, fresh
air was fluttering the curtains and drifting through
the room. The television was on . . . and the news
reporter was talking about the unidentified flying
object—the UFO—we saw the night before!

My eyes grew wide, and I started to speak. "That's what—"

"Hang on a minute," Mom said. We watched the news report and listened.

"*. . . witnesses say the object hovered over the water for several minutes before it shot up into the night sky and vanished. Several witnesses reported they saw a strange light come down from the object and pierce the water. So far, there's been no indication that anything unusual was spotted on radar, and it appears the sighting was an isolated incident. One witness who had his camera managed to get this photograph.*"

A picture suddenly flashed onto the screen. It was all black, except for the middle, which showed a blurry, colorful object. I recognized it instantly as the thing we'd seen the night before. However, the picture was so blurry that most people wouldn't know what it was. It could just as easily have been a photograph of a distant streetlight, for that matter.

The news reporter continued:

"*Officials are still searching for clues as to what the strange object could be. Some think it may have been a weather balloon that had been blown off course. Whatever it was, many people are scratching their heads this morning . . . and looking toward the sky. Alec Ramiro, reporting live for Channel 8 Eyewitness News.*"

"I told you I saw something last night!" I said. "Lots of people must have, or else it wouldn't be on the news!"

"But they think it might have only been a weather balloon," Dad said. "And that picture could have been a picture of anything. It certainly didn't look like a flying saucer."

I shook my head in defiance. "What we saw last night was *not* a weather balloon," I insisted. "There's no way. It had lights, and it shot up into the sky like a rocket!"

"Well, maybe they'll find out more later today," Mom said. "We'll have to keep an eye on the news."

"Yeah," Dad smirked. "Just in case we're invaded by aliens from another planet. We'll need to be prepared. And to think: I left my super-duper alien-fighting ray gun at home. Bummer."

I rolled my eyes.

At that very moment, we heard a sound that wasn't coming from the televison. It wasn't coming from another room in the hotel or in the hallway.

It was the distant sound of people screaming from the beach!

10

Dad and Mom shot up from the couch like they had been launched. They raced out onto the balcony, and I followed close behind.

Down by the shore, a small group of people had gathered. They had stopped screaming, but they appeared to be looking at something in the sand. I couldn't tell what it was, because they were too far away. But I hoped no one had been hurt.

"I wonder what happened," Mom said.

"Can't say," said Dad. "Hope everyone is all right."

"Breakfast!"

We turned to see Lee in his pajamas, standing near the television. He was carrying his teddy bear with one hand. That's what he normally does: as soon as he wakes up, he's hungry and wants to eat. He's an eating machine, that's for sure. And he always has his teddy bear with him until after breakfast. Then, he takes it to his bed and places it on his pillow. That's where the stuffed animal stays until it's time for him to go to bed again.

"Good morning, Lee," Mom said.

Lee looked around curiously. He was too little to grasp the concept of a hotel room. We had a refrigerator and a small kitchen-like area, but there wasn't anything else. If we wanted to eat, we had to go somewhere. Thankfully, the hotel we were staying at had breakfast for free in the lobby.

"Breakfast," Lee said again.

"We have to go to the lobby," Mom said, but Dad spoke up.

"I'll go down and bring back some things," he said. "Be right back."

While Dad was gone, I helped Lee change

out of his pajamas and into a pair of shorts and a T-shirt. I changed into a pair of shorts and a pink cotton blouse. The day was supposed to be hot, and I wanted to be sure we didn't wear something that would make us cook.

Dad returned with a tray of delicious food: cereal, apples, bananas, yogurt, muffins, orange juice, and milk. He placed the tray on the table.

"Some people down in the lobby were talking about some strange thing they saw on the beach a few minutes ago," he said. "That was what all the shouting was about."

"What kind of strange creature?" Mom asked.

Dad shook his head. "I'm not sure, and neither were they. They said it looked like some sort of weird jellyfish floating in the water. But they said it started to glow all sorts of colors, like it was lighting up. Then, it swam away."

"Jellyfish don't swim," I said. "Tony told me so."

"Well, whatever it was, they said it swam into deeper water and disappeared."

Strange, I thought. I'd never heard of

jellyfish that could light up. That was something I could ask Tony about, later today.

I soon forgot about jellyfish and flying saucers as I started to eat breakfast. There were too many fun things to look forward to: the amusement park, the water park, the Boardwalk, the beach . . . I wanted to make sure we didn't waste a single minute of the day. There was just too much fun to be had.

But very soon, I wouldn't be thinking about fun. I wouldn't be thinking about swimming in the ocean or walking the Boardwalk. I wouldn't be thinking about rides and slides and all the fun things that go on at Wildwood.

I would be thinking about more important things: like how to stay alive.

After breakfast, we cleaned up the hotel room a little. Dad breezed through one of the vacation brochures, looking for a place to have dinner that night. Lee took his teddy bear and placed it on his pillow. I had the job of putting sun screen on him, and he didn't put up a fuss. Then, I rubbed some on my arms, legs, neck, and face.

"How about we do this," Dad said as he placed the vacation brochure on the desk. "How about we walk the Boardwalk this morning, maybe hit the amusement park for a few rides. Then, we'll have lunch somewhere along the Boardwalk."

"Can we go to the water park after lunch?" I asked.

"Sure, that would be fun," Dad said.

Too cool! I thought. It was going to be a great day.

We left our hotel room. Within minutes, we were on the Boardwalk. That was one of the great things about staying at the hotel: we didn't have to get into our car and spend time driving anywhere. All of the attractions were right at our front door.

The Boardwalk was really a sight to see. It was mid-morning, and already there were people all over the place. It was a carnival-like atmosphere, with brightly colored arcades, souvenir shops, and whirling rides packed with people. The salty air was filled with dozens of smells: cotton candy, elephant ears, chocolate, hot dogs, coconut suntan oil, and more. People were smiling and laughing, splashing in the water park. A guy on stilts walked by us. He was wearing red and white striped pants, a blue shirt, and a red and white striped top hat. With the stilts, he must have been over ten feet tall! Not only was he walking with stilts, but he was juggling six bowling pins! We watched him for a moment and then continued on.

"Some place, huh?" Dad said.

"This is awesome!" I exclaimed.

We went to the amusement park. Mom and I went on rides together. Because Lee was so small, there were some rides he couldn't go on. But there were plenty more designed especially for littler kids, so he had a great time. So did Dad. Lee played some arcade games and even won a bag of glow sticks, which were cool. Each was about twelve inches long, and they came in a bunch of different colors. But when the stick was bent, it glowed brightly, like a light. Lee was completely enthralled.

For lunch, we ate hot dogs and walked along the Boardwalk. That's where we met up with Tony and Isobel.

They were riding their bikes along the Boardwalk. When I spotted them, I called out.

"Tony! Isobel! Over here!"

They heard my shouts, turned around, and rode up to us.

"Hey, Shayleen," Tony said.

"These are my friends I met yesterday," I said to Mom and Dad. "This is Tony, and this is Isobel." Of course, Dad had met Tony the day before, but he hadn't met his sister. Mom hadn't yet met either of them.

"It's nice to meet you both," Mom said. "Shayleen said she had a great time at the water park yesterday."

"That's where we're headed right now," Isobel said. "You wanna go with us?"

"Can I, Mom?" I asked.

"Sure," Mom said. "That's where we're headed, anyway. We have to go back to our room and get into our swimsuits, though."

"How about I meet you there in fifteen minutes?" I said to Tony and Isobel.

"We'll be there," Tony said. They rode off together and vanished into the throngs of people.

Suddenly, time seemed to stand still. A very odd feeling came over me. I was looking at everyone, all around, when I felt a strange wave of fear, for no reason at all.

I looked up into the perfect blue sky and at

the buzzing rides in the amusement park. I looked out over the beautiful blue ocean.

My fear grew.

What's the matter? I wondered.

I looked down the Boardwalk. Nothing was wrong, and there certainly wasn't anything to fear.

Yet, my horror continued to blossom to the point where I wanted to scream and run away. I felt like running to our hotel room and hiding in the closet. Anywhere to escape—

Escape what? What was I suddenly afraid of? Why was I feeling this way? Did it have something to do with what we saw last night or maybe what those people saw at the beach earlier in the morning?

I told myself I was only being silly, that it was only my imagination getting the best of me. I told myself there was nothing to worry about. So far, our vacation to Wildwood had been a great time.

So far.

But no longer. I was about to find out that, while we were having a good time, wandering around, seeing the sights, riding the rides, there were things going on—things that were approaching the beach—that we didn't know about.

Things *no one* knew about. Things no one could have possibly imagined.

And those 'things' were about to show themselves . . . in the worst possible way.

We returned to our hotel room and changed into our swimming suits. Although Lee had seemed excited to go to the water park, he was now content to play with his glow sticks. He'd bent two of them, and they glowed yellow and green.

"You'd better not bend all of them," I warned, "or else you won't have any more to play with. They won't glow forever, you know."

We all walked to the water park together. The day was steamy-hot, and I could see heat waves swirling up in the distance. It was a good thing we brought a lot of sun screen!

"I'm going to find Tony and Isobel," I said to Mom and Dad.

"Okay," Mom said. "But don't leave the water park. And come find us if you need more sun screen."

"I will," I said, and I skipped off, making my way through the throngs of people.

It took me a few minutes to find Tony and Isobel. Finally, I found them in line at a giant, red slide. It towered into the sky, twisting and turning downward and bending every which-way, finally ending at a large pool. I could hear shrieks of delight as people slid down, ultimately crashing with a huge splash in the pool.

"Shayleen!" Isobel called. *"Over here!"*

I turned to see her and Tony waving at me, and I ran up to them.

"Have you been on this slide, yet?" Tony asked.

I shook my head. "I missed that one yesterday," I replied.

"It's great!" Isobel said. "It's really, really fast!"

After riding the red slide a few times, Tony suggested we go to the wave pool. We had played in it the night before, and it was a lot of fun. It was like being in the ocean during a storm! The waves rolled up and down, swelling all around us, and we would sit on rubber rafts and try to hang on.

"I'll bet I can stand up on one!" Tony said as he climbed aboard his raft. "Watch!"

He stood, but as soon as the first wave welled up, he was tossed backward. He instantly lost his balance and plunged, laughing, into the water.

Isobel laughed. "Serves you right for bragging!" she said.

Tony broke the surface, sputtering and giggling.

Suddenly, there was a splash next to me in the water. Not a loud splash, but I thought maybe someone had tossed a beach ball.

I turned to see a large, green-blue blob. At first, I thought it was a plastic bag that someone must've thrown.

Then, I suddenly realized what it was.

A jellyfish!

Tony had told me how dangerous they were . . . and this one was only inches away from me!

The sun was hot, and the water was warm—but I froze.

Not because I was chilled or cold, but because I couldn't believe what I was seeing, and I was so horrified I don't think I could've moved if I tried.

Tony and Isobel saw the jellyfish.

"Shayleen!" Isobel screamed. *"Get away!"*

But I was too scared to do anything. I remained standing in water up to my neck, unable to move.

Tony, however, was quick to react. He grabbed my arm and pulled me away to safety.

"How did that thing get here?!?!" Isobel asked as the three of us moved farther away from the jellyfish. "They're only found in the ocean! They can't get into the water park!"

"It didn't sting you, did it?" Tony asked.

"If it had, I would have screamed like crazy," I said. "Thanks for pulling me away. I was so scared, I couldn't move a single muscle."

"But how did it get here?" Isobel asked again. We were about ten feet from the jellyfish, and we watched it warily. Other kids and some parents who had been in the wave pool saw it and were keeping other people away from it. Someone had summoned a lifeguard, and the lifeguard radioed for some help. Then, he ordered everyone out of the water.

"Did you see where it came from, Shayleen?" Tony asked as we reached the side of the wave pool and climbed out.

I shook my head, and my wet hair slapped my face. Water dripped from my chin and fingers. "I heard a splash in the water next to me," I replied. "I thought it was just a beach ball or something. When I turned, there it was."

"It was close enough to sting you, for sure," Tony said. "You're lucky. You could be on your way to the hospital right now."

I looked at the strange green-blue blob bobbing in the water. It looked like a discarded plastic bag, shining in the sun. But beneath the surface were long, dangerous tentacles—tentacles that could easily have stung me, and probably would have, if Tony hadn't pulled me away in time.

The wave machine had been shut off, and the water wasn't roiling and rolling like it had been. There were no people in the water, but a crowd had gathered around the edges of the pool. Everyone was staring curiously at the blob in the water.

Several workers arrived. One of them, a big man with no hair, carried a long net. He stood at the edge of the pool.

"Anyone hurt?" he called out. No one replied.

Then, he extended the net out . . . and what

happened next was like something out of a science fiction movie.

The jellyfish started to glow!

At first, it was just a blue-green color. Then, it changed to yellow and orange. Color seemed to roll through the floating bag like electricity.

A gasp rolled through the surprised crowd. But what happened next was not only unexpected—it was *unbelievable*.

The jellyfish was not only glowing . . . it began rising into the air like a balloon!

It was, by far, the most bizarre thing I had ever witnessed in my life. And, listening to the gasps of shock and surprise from onlookers, it was just as outlandish to them as it was to me. We watched as the glowing blob rose, its tentacles dangling below it. They, too, glowed different colors, and they swirled about like the tentacles of a squid. Water of various colors streamed from each tentacle, creating a multi-layered stain in the pool.

And, despite how frightening the episode was, no one ran away. Perhaps everyone was too shocked to believe what they were actually seeing.

The jellyfish continued to rise slowly, floating in the air. Its tentacles writhed and swirled like snakes.

"Do jellyfish do that?" I asked. Oh, I knew the answer already. I knew that jellyfish were restricted to water, and they certainly didn't fly or float in the air. I guess I just wanted someone to tell me out loud that what we were seeing wasn't supposed to be happening.

Isobel shook her head. *"No, they don't,"* she breathed. *"Nothing in the ocean does that."*

A hush fell over the crowd. I could still hear shrieks of laughter from other parts of the water park, but everyone around the wave pool had become silent. The bald park worker was still holding out his net, but he was staring wide-eyed as the jellyfish floated in the air above the pool. He, too, was just as shocked as everyone else.

And then, if *that* wasn't enough:

The jellyfish did another unexpected thing.

One of its tentacles began reaching out, and it seemed to be getting longer, like it was made out of rubber. At first, it appeared to be only a few feet long. In the next instant it had doubled in length and was rising up and rearing back like a cobra.

"We should get out of here," Tony said. "I don't like what's going on. That thing looks dangerous, like it might—"

Too late.

As Tony was uttering those words, the tentacle that had reared back suddenly sprang out with lightning speed . . . and it was aiming for me!

The glowing tentacle came at me like a javelin. Had I not been looking, it would have hit me square in the chest. Thankfully, I dodged to the right just in time—and the tentacle missed. It quickly retracted, but I didn't want to hang around to see what happened next. Neither did other people in the park. Most people started screaming and running for the exit. Other people in the park became alarmed, and they, too began leaving the rides and the water.

"Let's get out of here!" Tony shouted above

the screams of others. *"That thing is going to attack again!"*

There was a long line of people at the exit, all waiting to get out. Thankfully, there wasn't any pushing and shoving going on. But there were a lot of nervous glances. Everyone kept turning around to see where the bizarre, floating jellyfish was. I turned around, too . . . and it was a good thing I did. The jellyfish was no longer hovering above the wake pool, but drifting toward us, and fast! People waiting to get out started screaming and hollering.

"That thing is going to reach us before we get out of the water park!" Isobel shouted.

"Is there another exit?!?!" I said.

Tony shook his head frantically. "Only the one up ahead!" he replied.

"Well, we have to do something!" I cried, pointing at the jellyfish in the air, which was now picking up speed.

"Over there!" Isobel said, and she pointed to several small, aqua-colored buildings. There were paintings of colorful fish on the sides and the door. There were no windows.

"The changing rooms!" Isobel continued.

"We can hide in there!"

I turned once again, hoping the line of people leaving the exit had diminished. It had, but it would still be a few minutes before we would be able to get out . . . and by then, it might be too late. I couldn't imagine what it would feel like to have one of those sharp tentacles pierce my skin. Tony had told me the ones in the ocean were dangerous . . . but I'll bet they were *nothing* compared to the one hovering in the sky, coming at us!

And besides: even if we *did* make it out of the park, that didn't mean the jellyfish couldn't come after us. After all: the thing could *fly*. The thing could go anywhere!

"Go!" Tony shouted, and the three of us took off running toward the changing rooms. We had to be careful, too, because still more people were headed toward the exit, in the opposite direction. Twice, I ran into people, and I accidentally knocked over a little kid. His dad quickly snapped him up, and they kept running.

This isn't happening! I told myself as we sprinted. *It's like an alien invasion or something!*

Tony reached the changing room first. He slammed into the door and it burst open. He pushed inside, and Isobel followed. I was next, and I slammed the door behind me.

There wasn't much in the room other than a mirror, a table, and benches along the walls. On one wall was a row of green lockers, all of them with padlocks. The rest of the room was painted bright yellow, and, like the outside of the building, there were numerous fish painted on the walls. There were no windows, and the room was air conditioned and much cooler than the open air of the water park.

"We'll be safe in here," Tony said. "That thing won't be able to get us."

Outside, we could hear people shouting and screaming as they raced to the exit. I wondered where the flying jellyfish was and if it had tried to attack anyone else.

Soon, most of the shouting died off, and I figured the water park was empty. I didn't even hear any laughter or shouting in the distance. Everyone at the amusement park must have been evacuated, too.

"We can't stay in here forever," Isobel said. "We have to leave sometime."

"Maybe that thing is gone," I said. "Maybe it drifted into the sky and floated away."

"Only one way to find out," Tony said, and he strode to the door. Isobel and I followed him.

"Don't open it all the way," Isobel said. "Just enough so we can see outside."

Tony grabbed the metal door handle and slowly pulled the door open a tiny crack. We inched closer, peering over his shoulder, shocked at what we were now seeing . . . .

Jellyfish.

Not one.

Not two.

Not three or four.

Dozens of them.

They were hanging in the air like stationary balloons, their tentacles swirling and curling. They were glowing all sorts of bright colors—colors that changed and pulsated every few seconds. They were at varying heights, too. Some were high in the air—fifty feet or more. Others were only a few feet from the ground. There were a few in some of the numerous pools of water all around. If it had been something from a book or movie, it would have been cool.

But there was nothing cool about what we were seeing. What we were seeing was *real*. I knew it was, because I was seeing the things with my own eyes. So were Tony and Isobel.

"Where did those things come from?" Isobel asked.

"The thing we saw in the sky last night," I replied. "Remember? We saw that weird spaceship thing—or whatever it was—shoot a beam of light into the water before it zoomed off into space. I'll bet it had something to do with this!"

We watched in silence as the freaky jellyfish floated in the air. Some of them were rising up and down; others were moving forward and backward. All were glowing bright, neon-like colors.

"What do they want?" I wondered aloud.

"I don't even know what they *are*," Tony said. "I mean . . . they look like jellyfish, but they sure aren't *normal* jellyfish."

But what worried me more was the fact that

there were no people around, anywhere. It seemed everyone had left the water park, and, I was certain, the amusement park, too. No one wanted to be near the weird flying jellyfish.

We watched and listened. It was really strange: all day long, no matter where we went, we could always hear the sights and sounds of Wildwood: people laughing and howling with delight; happy, festive music; the steady hum of electric motors in the amusement park. Now, all we could hear was trickling water in the water park. Nothing else.

"Well," Tony said as he gently closed the door. "There's good news, and there's bad news."

Isobel put her hands over her face. "Give me the bad news first," she said.

"The bad news," Tony continued, "is that we're stuck here. With those things out there, in the sky and in the water, we can't leave this changing room."

"And what's the good news?" I asked.

"The good news is they can't get us," he replied. "All we have to do is stay here and wait. Our parents are going to know we're missing.

Someone, no matter what it takes, is going to come looking for us. We just have to stay here, and we'll be all right."

It was a good idea . . . but the jellyfish had ideas of their own.

We did the only thing we could do: we waited. Quietly, we wondered aloud about where the strange jellyfish could have come from.

"There's no such thing as flying jellyfish," Tony said. "In fact, they're not even a fish. They're more like a giant bug. They're supposed to just drift around in the water, waiting for fish to come by. I've never heard of one actually leaving the water, unless it was washed up on shore."

"These aren't normal jellyfish, for sure," Isobel said.

"This must have anything to do with the thing we saw in the sky last night," I said. "It was glowing all different colors, too . . . just like the jellyfish."

Tony scratched his head. "I don't know," he said. "But they sure are weird."

"It doesn't really matter, anyway," Isobel said. "Someone will help us. No one is going to let those things take over the park or hurt anyone."

We continued waiting, hoping to hear the voices of people approaching, alerting us that the jellyfish had gone away and it was safe to come out. The only thing we heard were a few birds chirping. We didn't even hear any seagulls calling out. I figured they, too, were staying clear of the water park and the mysterious flying jellyfish.

Five minutes passed, then ten.

Then fifteen.

No one came to help us.

"I wonder where everyone is," Tony said. "We can't wait in here forever. I'm going to see what's going on."

"You're going *out there?!?!*" Isobel asked.

"No," Tony said. "I'm just going to take

another peek. Maybe those things are gone."

Tony walked to the door, and Isobel and I followed. He pulled open the door a tiny bit. We huddled close and peeked over his shoulder.

The jellyfish were still in sight. However, in the distance, we saw that some of them had attached their tentacles to the neon lights in the amusement park. Many rides had tubes of light connected to them to give color, and they glowed brightly, even during the day. The jellyfish had wrapped their tentacles around these. The ones that had were glowing brighter than the rest and changing colors more rapidly.

"It's like they're feeding on the neon lights," Isobel whispered.

"Impossible," Tony said, shaking his head.

"So are flying jellyfish," his sister reminded him.

"At least most of them are far away from us," Tony said. "Maybe we could make a run—"

All of a sudden, Tony leapt back with such force that he sent Isobel and me flying. Both of us fell to the ground. I banged my head on one of the lockers, and it hurt. I placed my hand to my scalp and pulled it away. No blood, which was a good thing. But it still hurt.

Unfortunately, a bump on my head was the least of my worries.

The door was mostly closed, except for a thin opening. It was open because a long, green tentacle was trying to push its way inside!

"Help me close the door!" Tony wailed.

He sprang to his feet, and Isobel and I did the same. But the tentacle was writhing about, sliding farther and farther inside the room. Another tentacle, a yellow one, was also trying to wriggle in.

Tony attempted to push on the door, but the tentacle struck out at him. He was forced to leap away before it hit him. However, the tentacle withdrew a little, and that was the chance we needed. Isobel lunged forward and gave the door a swift kick with her right foot. I was surprised at how hard she hit it.

The door slammed closed . . . and the tentacle broke off! It snapped like a branch and fell to the floor, where it wiggled and flailed about like a live electrical wire.

"Keep back!" Tony shouted, and we bounded to the other side of the changing room.

With our backs to the wall, we watched the tentacle on the floor. It stopped moving after a few seconds, and glowing green slime—jellyfish blood, I guessed—was gushing out. Tendrils of smoke rose into the air.

"Holy cow!" Tony exclaimed. "That thing's blood is burning a hole in the cement floor!"

Tony was right! The blood seemed to be eating away at the floor, forming a bubbling hole! More goo trickled from the tentacle, and the pool of glowing green blood continued to burn the cement.

Now, that really wasn't a problem for us. We'd stopped the jellyfish from getting at us, and we'd broken off one of its tentacles.

The problem was the *smell*. There were no

windows in the small changing room, and the smell of the burning cement and green goo began to make us cough. My throat started to burn, and it became difficult to breathe. What we were breathing into our lungs was not good, and I knew it.

"Guys, we're going to be poisoned if we don't get some fresh air!" I said, gasping.

Isobel fell into a fit of coughing and gasping. Tony, too, was having a hard time. "Can't . . . can't breathe!" he stammered.

Because there were no windows, the only way out was the door . . . which we couldn't risk. That jellyfish was probably just on the other side, waiting for us. And it was probably mad, too, being that we cut off one of its tentacles.

I covered my mouth with my hands. I knew it wouldn't do much good, but I think that would be anyone's normal reaction. I glanced around, and I looked up.

I pulled my hand away from my mouth and pointed.

"Tony! Isobel!" I shouted. *"There's our way out, right there!"*

Tony and Isobel, still sputtering and coughing, looked up.

Above the table was a large, square air conditioning vent, covered by a white grill. I was sure it would be big enough for us to fit into. I was also sure we could remove the grill easily enough.

And with more and more poisonous gas filling the room, we didn't have a lot of time.

I climbed on top of the table and stood, where I was easily able to reach the vent. The grill pulled away without a problem, and I tossed it aside. It clanged to the floor.

Tony and Isobel climbed onto the table.

"Go!" Tony said. "I'll help push you up!"

I reached up into the vent. It was hard to pull myself up, because there wasn't much to grasp. However, there were ridges along the inside of the metal chute, and I was able to use my fingers. Tony and Isobel grabbed my feet and pushed, and I was able to climb up, where I found the vent made a sudden turn. Instead of going straight up, it bent sideways, like a horizontal tunnel. That would make things easier.

Isobel was next, and I turned and grabbed her hands. She climbed up easily, and we both turned and helped Tony up.

Still, the toxic gas from the burning green goo was getting to us. My eyes felt like they were on fire, and I was still coughing.

"This way!" I said, which was kind of a silly thing to say. After all: there was only one way we could go!

The vent was big, but it wasn't big enough for us to stand. We crawled along on our hands and knees, and every movement created loud, echoing booms from the straining sheet metal.

But the good news was that within minutes, we weren't coughing anymore, and I didn't smell any more of that awful, burning jellyfish blood.

Some vacation this turned out to be, I thought.

But we were on our way out, I was sure. Somewhere along the vent, there was bound to be another opening, and I knew we'd be safe. And besides: people must have known we were missing. I was sure my mom and dad were worried sick, and Tony and Isobel's parents, too. Maybe we weren't the only people trapped in the water park or the amusement park, and I was sure the police or someone was doing *something,* right at that very moment, to rescue us.

We continued to crawl through the noisy air conditioning vent. It was completely dark by now. Soon, we came to a place where the vent split. Oh, we couldn't actually *see* where it split, but, feeling around, I found one vent that went off to the right and one vent that went off to the left.

"Which way do we go?" Isobel said.

"I don't know," I said. "I've lost all sense of

direction. Any idea, Tony?"

"I don't know," Tony said. "But either one has to lead to somewhere in the park. And anyplace is better than being in that room with that stinky jellyfish tentacle. If we would have stayed there, I'm sure we would have been poisoned. I thought I was going to puke back there."

"Me, too," I said. "That was *awful.*"

We decided to follow the vent that went to the right, and we started out.

"I sure wish I could see," Tony said. "That would make things a lot easier." He was leading the way, and I was behind him. Isobel was behind me.

"At least those jellyfish can't get us," Isobel said. "Let's just be glad about that."

We banged along on our hands and knees. The noisy sheet metal groaned and buckled beneath our weight. We'd only been crawling for a minute or two when Tony shouted.

"Look!" he said. "There's an opening up ahead!"

I raised my head and looked. Sure enough,

I could see a faint, white glow ahead!

We would be safe, I was certain. I was sure that, wherever we were, we were away from those awful jellyfish. We would simply kick the grill out, drop down to the floor, and we would be safe. There might even be other people around to help us.

I was *sure*.

But, I've been wrong before, and I'll be wrong again.

Like this time.

We scrambled ahead on our hands and knees, our hopes surging.

We're getting out of here, I thought. Although our ordeal had started less than forty-five minutes ago, it felt like we'd been there all day. I couldn't wait to get out, to get somewhere safe. To see my mom and dad and Lee again.

We banged forward on the sheet metal. Tony stopped when he reached the grill. He pushed it with both hands, and it clanged to the floor below.

The three of us gathered around the opening. Below us was a room. There were no lights on, but there were windows, and we could see daylight streaming in. There were shelves filled with cleaning supplies, paper towels, and rags of all sorts. Several mops and buckets were leaning against the wall in a corner.

"A supply room," Tony said.

"Do you recognize it?" I asked.

Tony shook his head. "No," he said. "I don't really go into any of the supply rooms. Usually, the only people who go into these rooms are the workers."

Problem was, we were in the ceiling . . . and the floor was eight feet below us.

"I think I know what we can do," Tony said. "If we hang onto the ledge up here, we can lower ourselves down. It will still be a drop, but not as bad as if we were jumping from the ceiling."

"You first," Isobel said.

Tony rolled his eyes. "All right," he said. He grabbed the edge of the vent and placed his feet through the opening. Then, he dropped down, but his hands gripped the edge of the vent. He dangled for a moment, then let go.

He landed feet-first on the grill, but the force of the fall caused him to crumple to the ground.

"Are you okay?" Isobel called down.

Tony got to his feet. "It wasn't that bad," he said. "But there's a table over there, in the corner. I couldn't see it from where I was in the vent. I'll drag it under, so you guys don't have to fall like I did."

He disappeared for a moment. We heard scraping and screeching sounds, and he reappeared, pulling a large, wood table. He kicked the grill out of his way and dragged the table until it was directly beneath us.

"Come on down," he said. "Do like I did: hang onto the edge of the vent. Your feet should touch the table, and you won't have to drop."

Tony was right. Isobel and I were easily able to drop down onto the table without any problem at all. Then, we scrambled off the table and stood.

"Good news," Tony said as he looked out the window. "I don't see any of those weird flying jellyfish."

Isobel and I turned and looked through the glass. The window faced the ocean, and the only thing we could see was a blue sky with a few white, puffy clouds and the rolling, blue sea.

"Let's find our way out of here, then," I said.

There was only one door, and Tony opened it cautiously, wary that there could be a jellyfish on the other side. However, the door didn't lead outdoors. Instead, it led to an empty, unlit hallway.

"Follow me," Tony said as he entered the hall. "I think I know where we are."

Isobel and I did as Tony asked, and we followed him into the hall.

"I think we're in the maintenance building," Tony said. "I think I've been here before, with my dad. There should be a door up ahead that opens into the amusement park.

Tony was right. We found the door easily enough . . . but our hopes of escaping were shattered when we saw what was on the other side . . . .

21

We didn't even have to open the door to know our troubles weren't over. There was a thick glass window in the door, and, unfortunately, we saw exactly what we *didn't* want to see.

Jellyfish.

They were in the air, some high, some low. Most had their tentacles wrapped around the neon lights of the amusement rides.

"This is like a bad dream," Isobel said.

"Worse," I said. "I've never had a dream as bad as this."

The three of us stood at the door, staring. There were no people in sight, and because there were so many rides, tents, and food trailers, we couldn't see very far.

"Sooner or later," I said, "someone's going to come looking for us."

"The only problem is," Tony said, "they don't know where we are. Our parents think we're at the water park, which is way over there, on the other side of the Ferris wheel." He raised his arm and pointed. "We followed that air conditioning vent all the way here. If anyone's looking for us, they're probably looking in the wrong place."

I looked around. The jellyfish that had attached themselves to the neon lights were pulsating, growing brighter, then dimming, brighter, then dimmer. Isobel was right, I was sure: it was like the things were feeding on the lights.

"Look," Isobel said, pointing. "There's a walkie-talkie on that table over there."

Sure enough, there was a black and silver walkie talkie on a table beneath a blue and white striped tent. It had probably been left behind by one of the workers. Unfortunately, we couldn't get to it without leaving this building.

"That's what we need," Tony said. "But let's check this building. There might be a walkie talkie or a phone around here somewhere."

Isobel and I followed Tony down the hall. We found several doors, but they were all locked. We did find some that were open, but they were only storage rooms. There were no phones or radios anywhere.

"If we can make it to that radio, we can call for help," Tony said. "Then, at least someone will know where we are, and that we're safe."

"But we can't go out there while those things are around," Isobel said. "They'll attack us."

"Maybe I can run out there, grab the radio, and run back," Tony said. "Most of those things are moving around, not staying in one place. It would only take me a few seconds to get out there and back."

We walked back to the door and looked out the window. The scene was so strange. Here it was, a perfect day with a blue sky, a few clouds, and plenty of sunshine . . . but those weird jellyfish made the whole thing feel like a scary movie.

"See?" Tony said, motioning toward the window. "That radio really isn't very far."

I looked through the glass. The tent was about fifty feet away. The table with the radio was beneath it, in the shade. There were three metal garbage cans next to it.

"I don't know," Isobel said as she watched a red-colored jellyfish drift in the sky above the tent. The thing was slowly weaving back and forth. While we watched, it drifted over to the merry-go-round, where it attached itself to one of the bars of neon lights. The jellyfish grew very bright, and the neon light began to dim. There were other jellyfish doing the same thing: connecting to the lights, feeding off the neon. At least, that's what I *thought* they must be doing.

"Now's my chance," Tony said. "There aren't any close by. I'm a fast runner. I can make it to the radio, if I hurry."

He pushed the door open, looked up, and all around. "All clear," he said. "None of them are very close."

Isobel spoke quickly. "Tony, I still think that—"

But it was too late. Tony was already out the door, racing toward the blue and white striped tent and the radio on the table.

And Tony was right: he would make it to the radio.

Getting back was going to be the problem.

Everything went great . . . until Tony reached the
tent. He snapped the radio from the table and
turned around to begin sprinting back to us.

He didn't get far.

A jellyfish seemed to come from nowhere,
dropping out of the sky like a hawk. Tony hadn't
even left the tent when he found himself
confronted by the floating blob and its deadly
tentacles.

However, instead of running in the other
direction, Tony took a cautious step back. Then

another.

The jellyfish remained where it was, floating in the air.

Tony knelt down and ducked behind the three garbage cans.

"What's he doing?!?!" Isobel cried. "That thing is going to get him!"

"Maybe not," I said. "Maybe, if the jellyfish can't see him, it'll think he's gone away."

Seconds dragged on. We could no longer see Tony, as he was tucked behind the three garbage cans.

"He might be using the radio right now," I said.

"I hope so," said Isobel. "But I hope that thing doesn't see him."

The jellyfish started moving slowly. It hung in the air like a ghostly balloon, its tentacles swaying gently. From where we were, it looked harmless, like it might be some sort of new kite.

But we knew better. We didn't know where the things came from or why, but we knew they were anything *but* harmless.

The jellyfish lowered and began drifting

toward the three garbage cans. My heart began to beat faster, and I held my breath.

Did the jellyfish know Tony was hiding nearby? I wondered. *Did it know Tony was behind the three garbage cans?*

A single tentacle rose slowly. It reminded me of an Indian snake charmer I'd seen on television. The Indian sat on the ground, cross-legged, playing a horn-like instrument. In front of him was a woven basket. As the Indian played, he gently swayed side to side. Soon, a cobra rose slowly from the basket, seemingly entranced by the music and the swaying snake charmer. It had been fascinating to watch.

And that's what the jellyfish's tentacle reminded me of: a cobra, slowly rising, preparing to strike.

Isobel put her hands over her eyes. "I can't bear to watch," she said.

"Don't worry," I said, trying to ease her fear. "Tony is smart. He'll be all right."

I'm not sure I believed it myself. Oh, Tony was smart, for sure . . . but would he be all right? It was impossible to know.

In the blink of an eye, the jellyfish struck. The cobra-like tentacle lashed out and hit the middle garbage can, knocking all three of them over. Sparks flew from where the tentacle had hit the can. Their lids flew off, and garbage tumbled out.

Worse, Tony was now fully exposed. He was no longer hidden and was in full view of the jellyfish. He tried to get to his feet—but it was too late. Another tentacle rose into the air and shot out directly at him!

I didn't want to watch, but I didn't even have time to cover my eyes. That's how fast the jellyfish struck.

However, Tony was fast, too. There wasn't time for him to leap out of the way or to run, so he did the only thing he *could* do: he grabbed a garbage can lid by the handle and swung it in front of him like a shield.

The tentacle struck the lid. There was a popping sound and a shower of sparks . . . but Tony was safe. Just as he began to lower the shield and peer around it, the jellyfish struck with yet another tentacle. Again, there was a popping sound and an explosion of sparks.

Isobel dropped her hands from her face so she could see.

"He's using the garbage can lid as a shield!" I said.

While we watched, the jellyfish struck over and over. Soon, we noticed a curious thing was happening: the jellyfish was losing its color. Not only that, but it wasn't striking out so fast. It had become sluggish and tired.

"I think it's being drained of its energy," I said. "It looks like it's getting tired out."

Still, the jellyfish managed to lash out with a few tentacles. Soon, however, it had lost all color. It looked like a clear plastic bag floating in the air. Even its tentacles had lost their color.

Finally, the thing dropped out of the air. It plopped on the grass with a wet, gooey splat. Smoke began to rise into the air. The jellyfish didn't move.

That was the break Tony needed. However, instead of instantly running back to where we were, he picked up the other two garbage can lids and tucked them under his arm. Then, he sprinted as fast as he could toward us. Isobel opened the door and he flew inside. Then, she quickly closed the door.

Tony was out of breath from the short sprint.

"Man!" he exclaimed. "I thought that thing was going to get me for sure!"

"So did we!" I said. "That was smart thinking, using that garbage can as a shield!"

"I didn't have any other choice," Tony said, still gasping for breath. "I'm just glad I was able to reach it in time. But did you see what happened?" he asked. "The more that thing hit the can with its tentacles, the weaker it got." He handed one garbage can lid to me, then gave one to his sister. "We can use these," he said. "They can be our shields, if one of those things attacks."

"And if it keeps attacking and attacking, like that last one," Isobel said, "it will use all its energy and die."

"Were you able to radio for help?" I asked.

Tony shook his head. "The radio was dead."

"So, we're no closer to being rescued than we were five minutes ago," Isobel said.

"Yeah, but at least we're safer, now. We've got some protection with these garbage can lids. If one attacks us, we can deflect the tentacles by using the lids as shields."

All of that seemed fine . . . but at that precise moment, the glass in the door exploded and flew everywhere. Shocked, we could only stand there as a single, wiry tentacle appeared, writhing and coiling like a downed electrical wire!

It took a moment to grasp what was happening. A jellyfish had used its tentacles to shatter the window in the door . . . and now it was attacking! It was big, too . . . bigger than most of the ones we'd seen so far. It glowed a bright, blood red, except for its tentacles, which changed colors from yellow to green.

And it was a good thing Tony had thought to grab the garbage can lids! If it hadn't been for those, we would've been goners. The jellyfish kept striking and striking and not with one tentacle, but five or six! Still, we somehow managed to use the lids as shields and deflect each attack. Sparks flew when a tentacle hit the metal lid.

We tried to back away, too, but the jellyfish came after us. It drifted through the broken window. Some of its tentacles just sort of dragged along; others were more active, and they moved around like animated arms and legs.

But the good thing was that it was weakening. Every time a tentacle hit one of our garbage can lids, the jellyfish seemed to fade in color. Even as we backed down the hall while the thing was still after us, it seemed to be losing strength. It wasn't floating as high in the air, and its colors were becoming dull and bland. Soon, it didn't even have the energy to attack any more. It sank slowly to the ground, where it appeared to melt. Green goop began pouring out onto the floor, and, like the one in the changing room, it began to burn a hole in the floor. Once again, we were overcome with a putrid, toxic smell.

"Let's go back to the room where we came in through the vent," Tony suggested. "We can plan what do to from there. We'll be away from this stinky thing, and we'll probably be safer."

We left the decomposing jellyfish in the middle of the hall and walked back into the supply room. I closed the door behind me.

Through the window, we could see the ocean and the sky . . . and jellyfish. There were only a few of them, but they were a reminder that we still weren't out of danger.

"It's strange how the garbage can lids cause them to die off," Isobel said.

"The metal must cause some sort of weird reaction," Tony said. "And the way their green blood burns the ground! It's like they're nuclear or something."

"How would they become nuclear?" I asked. "That just sounds impossible."

"I don't know," Tony replied, shaking his head. "And they might not actually *be* nuclear. But whatever they are, I've never seen anything like them before. And I don't think anyone else has, either."

"We have to get out of here," Isobel said. "That's all there is to it."

I pointed to the window. "But Isobel, those

things are all over the place."

"But that one came through the window in the door," she said. "They'll do it again. We *have* to get out of the park to somewhere safe."

"If there even *is* any safe place," I said glumly.

"My sister's right," Tony said. "We have to get out of here. Right now, we're safe. But what if three or four of those things come at us? They could trap us in this room, and we'd never be able to fend them off, even with our garbage can lids."

"So, what are you suggesting?" I asked.

"I say we make a run for it," Tony said. "We've got these lids, and they've worked good so far. I say we take our lids and make a run for the park exit. If a jellyfish attacks, we'll deal with it. It's better than waiting around here to have them come after us."

Isobel and I were silent as we thought about what Tony was saying. Sure, we'd be out in the open if we left the building, and a jellyfish could attack us. Or two or three. But, it would be better than having them attack us here in the building. Of course, there was a chance we wouldn't get attacked at all. Then, we could reach the exit . . . and be safe. I knew Mom and Dad were probably worried sick about me.

Then, I had another thought.

What if something happened to Mom and Dad? What if one of those things got them?

I pushed thoughts like that out of my mind. I had other things to worry about, and if I didn't keep a clear head, there was no way we were going to get out of this alive.

"I say we go for it," Isobel finally said. "Like Tony said: we can't stay here. Sooner or later, those things are going to come after us. Then, we'll be trapped."

Reluctantly, I decided to go along. Tony's plan wasn't a *bad* one . . . but I wasn't really thrilled about going out into the open while those things were still out there.

"Okay, let's do it," I said, not realizing what we were soon going to be up against.

The only way out was through the door with the broken window. We left the supply room and walked cautiously through the hall, each of us holding our breath so we wouldn't have to smell the poisonous fumes of the decaying jellyfish. When we saw it, it hardly resembled a jellyfish at all. What was left was simply a puddle of dirty, smoldering goop that was burning a hole in the floor.

Tony reached the door first, and he let out the breath he'd been holding and took in the fresh air coming through the broken window. Isobel and I followed, and we both gulped down the fresh air. We could still smell the rotting jellyfish coming from the hall, but it wasn't so bad.

"We'll go slow," Tony said, "and try to stay in the shadows. Don't run out in the open unless you absolutely have to. And whatever you do, don't lose your garbage can lid!"

I was glad Tony was with us. He'd taken control. I'm sure he was just as frightened as Isobel and I, but he didn't let it show.

"Where are we going to go first?" Isobel asked.

Tony pointed. "Over there," he said. "The exit is that way, so we'll head to the tilt-a-whirl. There aren't any jellyfish near it right now, and there are lots of places to hide all around it. See the tent and the trailer? Both will give us cover if we need it. You guys ready for this?"

Isobel looked at me. I must've had a worried expression on my face, because she looked at me curiously. "Are you all right?" she asked.

"I'm fine," I said. "But I'm a little scared and nervous."

"Me, too," she said. "But we'll be okay."

I smiled thinly. "I hope so," I said.

Tony pushed the door open and gave a quick glance in all directions. We could still see numerous jellyfish, but most were some distance away, attached to neon lights on the rides.

"Let's go," Tony said. "Remember: hang onto your garbage can lids."

Which was good advice, because we were going to need them a lot sooner than we thought.

We set out in single file for the tilt-a-whirl, moving slowly and stealthily, like three cats approaching a bird.

We never made it.

When we were halfway there, a movement to the right caught my attention. It was a jellyfish, all right. It had spotted us. It moved slowly and cautiously, stalking us in that wary, careful way a wolf stalks its prey.

"There's one, right there!" I said, raising my garbage can lid to prepare to defend myself. Tony

and Isobel turned, and they, too, readied their shields.

"Let's keep walking," Tony said. "Just be ready with your lids."

We continued walking single file toward the tilt-a-whirl. All the while, we had our shields raised up, waiting for the jellyfish to strike.

But when we *were* finally attacked, we weren't prepared.

The reason?

It was *another* jellyfish that attacked us!

I saw it in the air ahead, moving quickly toward us. It was moving so fast that I didn't even have a chance to warn Tony. Thankfully, he had spotted the movement and quickly swung his shield around in front of him. He was just in time, too, because the jellyfish had already unleashed one of its harpoon-like tentacles. It struck the garbage can lid with a metallic *ping!* and sparks bloomed, flower-like, before falling to the ground and burning out.

But that left the other jellyfish poised to strike Isobel and me—and it did, using three tentacles at the same time.

"Watch out!" I screamed as the tentacles came at us like javelins. One struck Isobel's garbage can lid in a shower of colorful sparks.

But two tentacles came at me. I thought I was prepared, but the two tentacles hit with such force they knocked the lid right out of my hands! There was a loud pop, a rain of sparks, and the garbage can lid was suddenly knocked from my hand! It landed in the grass several feet away and rolled to a stop.

"Shayleen!" Isobel screamed.

I was defenseless, and I knew it. Without my garbage can lid to serve as a shield, I wouldn't have any protection against the jellyfish's attacking tentacles. Even if I tried to run away, I knew the jellyfish would be faster.

So, I sprang for the lid, hoping to pick it up before the jellyfish struck.

"Shayleen!" Isobel repeated . . . just as I tripped over my own feet and fell to the grass.

The jellyfish must have sensed I was powerless, because it floated closer to me, and a tentacle shot out.

My garbage can lid, however, was out of

reach, and there was no way I could reach it in time. I closed my eyes and waited for the worst.

It was quick thinking on Tony's part that saved my life.

He was still fighting the jellyfish that was attacking him, but he saw the trouble I was in. In one swift motion, he threw his shield sideways into the air . . . right in front of me. There was a familiar metallic *pop!* sound as the tentacle struck the garbage can lid. Sparks flew, and the lid was knocked to the ground—but Tony had succeeded. He'd thrown his own shield to deflect the tentacle that, no doubt, would have hit me.

But our ordeal was far from over. Both jellyfish showed no signs of letting up their attacks. Without thinking twice, I reached down and picked up the lid Tony had thrown. Tony had already picked up the lid the jellyfish had knocked from my hand.

And the fight raged on. Tentacle after tentacle came at us, but we were able to use the garbage can lids and deflect each assault. And the more the jellyfish attacked, the weaker they became.

"They're done for!" Isobel said triumphantly as one of the jellyfish slowly sank to the ground, depleted of color and energy. It bubbled and hissed in the grass. Smoke rose.

Isobel and I turned to help Tony, but he seemed to be doing fine on his own. The jellyfish attacking him was quite weak and could no longer attack with much aggression. Soon, it too was nothing more than a pile of wet blubber in the grass.

"Look!" Isobel said, pointing to the sky.

Several more jellyfish appeared, glowing different colors, flashing like brilliant strobe lights.

"Over to that trailer!" Tony shouted, pointing. Not far away was a cotton candy stand, lit with colorful neon lights. Someone had left in a hurry, as the door was wide open.

We raced to it and flew inside. I was the last one in, so I grabbed the door and slammed it closed behind me.

Very quickly, however, we realized our mistake. The jellyfish, of course, were capable of shattering glass with their tentacles. The glass windows of the cotton candy stand were much thinner than the glass in the door window had been, and the jellyfish that had attacked had no trouble breaking it with a single tentacle.

We watched, horrified, as nearly a dozen jellyfish descended from the sky like ghosts, surrounding the tiny trailer.

It was an ambush . . . and there was nowhere for us to go.

The jellyfish were all around the trailer, surrounding us, glowing brightly. Had I not been so terrified, I'm sure I would have been fascinated by their radiating bodies.

But I knew how dangerous and powerful they were. I also knew there were more of *them* than us . . . and I also knew they could break windows. If those jellyfish wanted to get at us, there was nothing we could do to stop them.

"Maybe this wasn't such a good idea after all," Tony whispered as we watched the jellyfish. They

remained a few feet from the trailer, suspended in the air like a child's mobile.

We kept our garbage can lids raised, just in case we had to defend ourselves. The jellyfish showed no signs of coming after us, but that could change in an instant.

"It's like they're waiting and plotting," Isobel said. "I wonder if they can communicate with each other."

"I don't know," I said. "I hope not."

"They seem to know what they're doing," Tony said. "Somehow, they must be communicating with each other in some way."

"They don't have any mouths or eyes," I said. "They must be talking to each other through brain waves or something."

"It doesn't look like they have any brains," Isobel said.

"Maybe not brains in the way we would imagine them," Tony said. "But they have tentacles, and they know how to use them."

The jellyfish began to move. It was as if some unseen signal was given, some unknown code only the jellyfish could understand. We watched as they slowly began drifting closer and closer to the trailer, closing in on us.

"Be ready," Tony said. "If those things come through the windows, we won't have any choice but to make a run for it."

The jellyfish drifted closer and closer. Their movements were smooth and calm, deliberate. Soon, they were only inches from the windows.

I was so scared I couldn't breathe. My heart was hammering in my chest, and I thought it was going to explode. I knew that at any moment, snake-like tentacles would smash the glass windows and wriggle inside the trailer. Tony had told us to be ready to run, but I knew there was no escape. Not this time. Not if the jellyfish attacked. There were too many of them, all around the trailer.

"Let's get out now," Isobel whispered. Her voice quaked with fear. "Let's get out while we still can."

"Let's wait a second," Tony said. "They're up to something."

"Yeah," I said. "They're up to the windows. Next thing, they'll be breaking in here, and we're going to be done for."

"No, something else is going on with them," Tony said. "Look."

While we watched, the jellyfish began to rise. Soon, we could no longer see their bubble-like bodies . . . only their tentacles were visible. Then, the tentacles vanished, too.

"Are they gone?" Isobel asked.

She was answered by a strong buzzing sound and a strange feeling of electricity in the air.

"What's that?" I asked.

"I think I know," Tony said as he took a cautious step toward the window. He peered up, and his eyes grew wide. Then, he looked at us. *"The jellyfish are attached to the neon lights on the trailer!"* he hissed. *"They're sucking all the neon juice from the lights!"*

"What if we shut the power off?" I wondered aloud. "Then, they wouldn't have any neon to eat."

Tony looked at me with an expression of surprise. "You know . . . that's a great idea! If we kill the power to the lights, maybe they'll go away!"

"Maybe they'll eat us, instead," Isobel said

glumly.

"They might do that, anyway," Tony said. "Let's try shutting off the power. There has to be some sort of light switch in here. Help me find it."

The three of us, still holding onto our garbage can lids, scrambled around the trailer, looking for the switch. We found several switches that turned off the lights and power inside the trailer, but nothing turned off the lights on the outside.

Finally, Isobel found a gray panel door in the wall. When she opened it, she found a row of black switches arranged vertically, all except for one. It was at the top of the inside panel.

"This says 'main,'" Isobel said. "Is this it?"

"That's it!" Tony said, rushing to her side. He reached out and flicked the switch.

Instantly, all power in the trailer went off. The strange feeling of electricity vanished, and the odd buzzing stopped.

But what happened to the jellyfish was another matter altogether . . . .

In the seconds after Tony had flicked the switch and cut the power to the trailer, the jellyfish started *exploding!* They sounded like dull firecrackers going off all around the trailer. Colorful goop flew everywhere: it splattered on the grass and cement outside the trailer, and it stained the windows and began running down in goopy streams.

"What's happening?" Isobel asked. Her eyes darted around anxiously.

"They're blowing up!" Tony said.

"Something must have happened when I turned the power off!"

It took only a few seconds for all of the jellyfish to explode. More colorful goop—jellyfish blood and guts, I imagine—coated the outside windows. The stuff actually began to melt the glass, and smoke rose into the air. Once again, we began to smell the now-familiar toxic jellyfish gas. But now we had another problem: the goop began burning through the walls and the ceiling of the trailer! It started dripping down all around us!

"Don't let it touch you!" Tony shouted. *"That stuff is like nuclear acid! It'll probably burn right through our skin!"*

The stuff was really gushing in now, and we had no choice but to get out of the trailer. I pushed the door open and bounded outside, followed by Isobel and Tony. Thankfully, there weren't any jellyfish nearby. The only ones I could see were in the distance, either attached to neon lights or hovering above them.

We turned to look at the trailer. Thick wisps of smoke were rising into the air. The jellyfish goop was bubbling and hissing. We could still smell the awful stench of the burning jellyfish goop, but it wasn't nearly as strong as it was inside.

Soon, the entire trailer was collapsing in on itself. We heard loud screeches and crunching as plastic, fiberglass, wood, metal, and glass crashed to the ground.

"We got out of there just in time," Isobel said. "If we would've stayed in there a minute longer, we would've been fried."

Then, we heard *another* noise.

A whirring, drumming sound, far away. But it grew louder quickly, and, although we couldn't see it, we instantly knew what it was.

"That's a helicopter!" I shouted.

Suddenly, it appeared in the sky, swooping over us. I don't think I've ever been so happy and relieved in my life! All along, I had been wondering when help would come, when someone would save us . . . and here they were! We were going to be rescued! Someone was finally coming to save us!

The helicopter flew directly over us. It was white and blue, and it looked like a police helicopter. It was so close, I could see the pilot! He was looking down at us while talking into a radio headset.

We started waving and jumping up and down.

"Help! Help us!" we shouted, which wasn't really necessary. The pilot could see us, and I knew it would only be minutes before he set down the helicopter. Then, we would climb aboard and fly off. We would be safe.

But the jellyfish weren't going to let that happen.

30

As the helicopter made a sweeping bank to turn around, seven or eight jellyfish began drifting toward it. At first, they moved slowly. Then, as if an unseen signal was given, the jellyfish lunged toward the flying helicopter, attaching themselves to the landing runners and to the side of the chopper itself.

Suddenly, the helicopter began veering violently about, jerking to the left and then back to the right. Clearly, the pilot was losing control.

"Oh, no!" I shouted as the helicopter buzzed

over our heads. Whatever the jellyfish were doing, it was causing big trouble for the helicopter pilot. The craft darted up, then down, then sideways. The thundering of the spinning blades was so loud, I could feel it through my whole body.

"He's going to crash!" Tony shouted. *"The jellyfish are going to cause him to crash!"*

The helicopter came dangerously close to the Ferris wheel before banking skyward again. The jellyfish were still attached to the fuselage and showed no sign of letting go.

This is a nightmare, I thought. *This is the worst nightmare I've ever had.*

Of, course, it *wasn't* a nightmare . . . and that's probably what made the whole thing even *worse.*

The helicopter dipped from view behind the rides, and we heard a heavy splash as the craft crashed into the ocean. The thundering chop of the whipping blades stopped suddenly, and we knew it was the end of the line for the helicopter and the pilot.

"That was our last hope," Isobel said. Sadness weighed heavily in her voice. She sounded like she'd given up.

"No," Tony said, shaking his head. "We're going to get out of here. We're not going to be outsmarted by a bunch of colorful blobs."

"But how, Tony?" Isobel said.

"I don't know," Tony replied. "But we'd better get someplace where we're not out in the open. If we keep standing here, we're going to be sitting ducks."

"There's a washroom, over there," I said, pointing.

"That's as good a place as any," Tony said. "Let's go."

We ran to the washroom and closed the door behind us. Inside, there were several stalls and a row of sinks with a mirror. When I saw myself, I gasped. My T-shirt was dirty, and my hair was a mess.

I shrugged it off. Normally, I wouldn't have gone out of the house if I looked like that. But right now, I was lucky to be alive, and it didn't really matter if I looked like a ragamuffin.

A big, white wastebasket stood near a sink, and Tony pushed it in front of the door.

"Just in case one of those things tries to get in," he said. "Now . . . let's put our heads together. We've got to figure a way to get out of here."

We thought and thought, each of us quietly glancing at the floor, the walls, the ceiling. Far in the distance, we heard a siren wail. Then, it fell silent.

"Well, at least someone knows we're here," I said. "Everyone else must've made it out of the park, but someone must know that there are three kids trapped inside. Help will be on the way soon, I bet."

"Not after what happened to that helicopter," Tony said. "They're not going to do anything risky. If we're going to get out of here, we're going to have to do it on our own."

We remained silent, thinking. Like the changing room, there were no windows in the washroom, so we couldn't see outside. Hopefully, that meant the jellyfish couldn't see us, and they wouldn't know we were here.

I thought and thought, but nothing came to me. If we made a run for the exit, I was sure the jellyfish would be all over us, just like they had done to the helicopter. Even if we waited here, the jellyfish might find out where we were and attack. I didn't know what they wanted from us, and I didn't care. All I knew was they were nasty, and they wouldn't have any problem destroying us, if they could. With tentacles that could shoot out like arrows, we wouldn't have a chance. Even if we *were* successful in destroying them, we had to be careful to stay away from them. At the cotton candy trailer, we'd found that their blood was like nuclear acid, and it ate through everything.

A sudden thought raced through my head.

My eyes grew, and my body stiffened. Tony and Isobel saw this, and they looked at me.

"What is it?" Isobel asked.

"That's it!" I said, nearly shouting. "We don't have to get out of here! I know what we can do to stop those things, once and for all!"

Tony and Isobel looked at me, and I began to explain my idea.

"When we shut off the power in the cotton candy trailer," I said, "it did something to the jellyfish. All of the ones touching the neon lights exploded. Well, if we can shut off the power to the whole amusement park, the jellyfish touching the neon lights would probably do the same thing: blow up."

Tony thought about this. "That's not a bad idea," he said. "I think I know where the main power box is, but we'd have to get to it without getting attacked by those things."

"We have our garbage can lids," I said, holding mine up. "Sure, they're not the best protection, but they've worked pretty good, so far."

"But, don't you think it would be better to wait?" Isobel asked.

"If you would have asked me that a half hour ago," I said, "I would've said 'yes.' But you saw what those things did to that helicopter. No one is going to try to save us if they know they're going to be attacked by jellyfish. In fact, they might not think we're still alive."

"Shayleen's right," Tony said. "If we wait, the only thing we're doing is giving the jellyfish more time to get us. I'd rather take my chances and try to zap them by killing the power to the whole amusement park. It might not get rid of every single one, but it will take care of most. In fact, I'll go alone, and you two can stay here. That way, all three of us won't be in danger."

I shook my head. "No," I said, "we all go together. That way, we can look out for each other. If I had been by myself when that jellyfish knocked the lid from my hands, I wouldn't be here talking about this. I say we stick together, so we can protect one another."

Isobel nodded. "All right," she said. "I say we do it. I want those things to blow up, and I want to go home."

Tony walked to the garbage can, dragged it to the sink, and opened the door a few inches. He peered outside.

"The only jellyfish I see are attached to the neon lights," he said. "I'm sure there are more around, though. You guys ready?"

"Let's do it," I said, and Isobel nodded in agreement.

"Follow me, and keep your eyes to the sky," he said. "If we get attacked by a bunch at the same time, we're going to be in a lot of trouble. But I don't think that'll happen."

Unfortunately for us, what Tony *thought* would happen and what was *about* to happen were two totally different things.

Why is it things are never as easy as they seem? I mean . . . I knew we were up against a lot. I guess I just figured it wouldn't be that difficult to make it to the main power panel, shut the power off, and watch the jellyfish cook like burnt marshmallows.

Then again, maybe I was just being too hopeful, too optimistic. Maybe I just thought the plan would work, and our ordeal would soon be over.

Wrong.

When we opened the door and left the

washroom, we quickly learned our ordeal had just begun. There were jellyfish of all sizes and colors floating in the sky, behind trees, everywhere. As soon as we were out in the open, one of them descended on us.

"There's one, right there!" I shrieked, pointing skyward. *"He's coming after us!"*

"Run over to that white building!" Tony shouted as he pointed. "That's where the main offices are. I'll be right behind you!"

Isobel and I took off running, swinging our garbage can lids at our sides. Tony ran closely behind us, but he kept watch as the jellyfish came closer and closer.

Suddenly, I heard the now-familiar metallic pinging of a tentacle striking a garbage can lid. I turned around. The jellyfish had descended close to the ground and was lashing out at Tony. Tony had stopped, and he was using his garbage can lid to ward off the attack. While he shielded himself from the tentacles, he walked backward.

"Keep going!" he shouted. *"I can handle this one! Keep running and don't stop until you get inside the main office building!"*

I didn't want to leave him there all alone, but he looked like he was handling the jellyfish without too much difficulty. Already, the creature seemed to be losing color and strength. Hopefully, Tony would be able to defeat it and follow us to the building.

Isobel and I continued to run, weaving around rides and food stands. It seemed strange to be in such a big amusement park on such a beautiful day with no people around at all. There was no happy music playing. The neon lights were on, but none of the rides were operating. The entire park had been deserted.

Isobel reached the main office building first. She grabbed the doorknob and pulled, and the door flew open. I followed her indoors and quickly pulled the door closed.

There was a large window off to the right, and we went to it and looked outside. Not far away, we saw Tony. His back was toward us, and he was still fending off the jellyfish, which was now so weak that most of its tentacles dragged the ground. The hulking bubble that had been a bright orange was now a dirty brown. It would be only a matter of moments before it collapsed to the ground.

And that's when a bright red and green jellyfish suddenly sank from the sky, right behind him!

Isobel gasped.

"Tony!" I screamed. *"Behind you! There's one right behind you!"*

Tony kept walking backward. Obviously, he couldn't hear me.

"Tony!" I shrieked again.

It was no use. Tony was only a few feet away, and he was so focused on the jellyfish in front of him that he didn't know there was one behind him, too.

And he was going to walk right into it!

Without wasting another second, I bolted for the door and threw it open.

"TONY!" I screamed as loud as I could. At the same time, I let the garbage can lid fly.

Tony spun just as the red and green jellyfish attacked with a long, glowing tentacle. Just in the nick of time, he'd heard my shout and was able to swing his garbage can lid in front of him to deflect the tentacle.

A split second later, the garbage can lid I'd thrown struck the red and green bubble of the jellyfish, and the effect was instant. There was a shower of sparks that looked like fireworks going off. The jellyfish fell to the ground in a hissing, spitting blob of goop. Wisps of smoke boiled and rose.

Tony didn't waste any more time. He darted around the steaming pile of bubbling goop and ran toward the building, and he didn't stop until he was inside. I leapt in behind him and slammed the door.

"Good . . . good . . . think . . . thinking," he said as he gasped for breath. "If you hadn't warned me in time, that thing would've got me."

I looked out the window. What was left of the jellyfish wasn't much. It looked like someone poured two big piles of melted plastic on the grass and cement. Already, some of the liquid goo was burning through the pavement and scorching the grass, turning it black.

"I think the electric panel is in a back room in this building," Tony said. He'd finally caught his breath, and he started walking down the hall, carrying his garbage can lid. Isobel, carrying her garbage can lid, followed, and I followed her.

The floor was blue carpet, and the walls were painted flat white. We passed several open doors. Some of the rooms contained desks stacked with papers. In one, Tony saw a phone. He strode inside and picked it up. He put it to his ear for a moment, then he shook his head and put it down. "No dial tone," he said. "The phones must be out."

He returned to the hall, and we continued walking.

"What's the power box look like?" Isobel asked.

"It's a gray metal panel, built into the wall," Tony replied. "I think Dad showed it to me once. I remember him opening it up and telling me that, if they needed to, they could shut down the whole amusement park with a single flick of a switch. It's called the 'main breaker,' and he told me to stay away from it, because it's dangerous."

"Why is it dangerous?" I asked.

"Because there's so much electricity," Tony said.

"So, if Dad finds out that we're going to shut off the main power, we're going to be in big trouble," Isobel said.

"In case you haven't noticed," Tony replied, "we're *already* in big trouble. This is our only chance to wipe out a bunch of those things all at once."

Somewhere in the building, we heard glass shattering. We stopped walking and listened.

"Where did that come from?" Isobel whispered.

"Somewhere in the building," Tony replied.

"It was one of those things, I bet," I said quietly.

We started walking again, and we continued until the hall split: it continued to both the left and the right. Tony looked both ways, then pointed to the left.

"I think it's down there," he said, "but I can't be sure. It's been a few years since I've been back here."

He walked quickly, and Isobel and I hurried after him. We passed more offices and rooms; most of the doors were closed, and there were name plates posted on them.

"It's back here," Tony said. "I remember now."

Just as he was about to turn and walk into a room on the right, he stopped so quickly that Isobel and I bumped into him.

We looked into the room. On the far wall was a large, gray metal panel, just like Tony had described.

And right next to it, floating in the air like a ghost, was a jellyfish.

"I knew this wasn't going to be that easy," I whispered.

"Nothing about this whole day has been easy," Isobel whispered back.

We stood in the doorway. The jellyfish was a shiny blue color, and its tentacles were blood-red. Like all the other jellyfish, it appeared to be glowing. It was on the other side of the room, but Tony and Isobel raised their garbage can lids, just in case the thing attacked with its tentacles. The ground was littered with hundreds of glass particles: the jellyfish had broken through the window. Now we knew the cause of the shattering glass we'd heard only moments before.

"It's almost as if it knew we were coming here," Tony said quietly. *"It's like the thing is waiting for us."*

"Now what?" Isobel asked.

"We need to get to that electric panel," Tony said. *"We need to create a diversion and lead the jellyfish away."*

At that moment, the jellyfish began drifting toward us. We took a step back. Isobel and Tony were in front of me with their garbage can lids, but I still didn't feel safe. Something told me if that thing wanted to get all three of us at once, it could.

We backed up against the opposite wall in the hall. Meanwhile, the jellyfish drifted closer to us and away from the panel.

"Here's what we'll do," Tony said. "I'll go this way down the hall. Isobel . . . you and Shayleen go that way. That thing is bound to follow one of us. Whoever has the first opportunity to get into the room and shut the power off, do it!"

Shayleen and I backed away. I stood behind

her, and she held her garbage can lid up, ready to deflect any attack by the jellyfish. Tony did the same thing, except he went the other way.

The jellyfish emerged from the room and entered the hallway, and we kept back-stepping. The thing stopped and hung in midair, as if it was confused. It slowly turned one way, then back.

Then, it headed down the hall toward Tony.

Isobel and I stopped walking and watched.

"We'll wait for it to get a little farther away," Isobel said. "Then, I'll go into the room to the electric panel."

"I'm going with you," I said. "If you leave me, I won't have any protection against that thing. Or any others, if they show up."

"Okay," Isobel said. "Then, I'll cover for you while you open the panel and shut the power off."

That sounded like a good plan . . . especially since the jellyfish was still following Tony. It hadn't attacked yet, but we knew it was only a matter of moments.

"Come on," Isobel said, and she started walking back to the room where the electrical panel was. I followed her closely. Our eyes never left the shiny blue jellyfish that was following her brother.

"Hurry it up!" Tony shouted. *"This thing is going to start attacking!"*

Isobel and I reached the door and turned into the room.

"I'll stay here," Isobel said. "Go and shut off the main power switch."

With Isobel standing guard at the doorway, I raced across the room to the gray panel. I threw it open, revealing four rows of dozens of black switches. At the top of the rows was a single, large, black switch. An inscription in the metal beneath it read: MAIN.

Using two fingers, I pulled the switch. There was a loud *snap!* . . . but, other than that, nothing happened—for a moment.

Suddenly, we heard explosions outside. They came from all around, it seemed.

"It's working!" Isobel shouted. "Shayleen did it!"

I listened to the sounds of exploding jellyfish, knowing our ordeal was nearly over. Oh, sure, I knew we still would have to deal with any jellyfish that weren't touching the neon lights . . . but I didn't know one of those jellyfish was drifting through the broken window at that very moment . . . .

I never saw the tentacle coming.

I was still standing by the electrical panel, listening to the continuous explosions all around the amusement park.

Suddenly, there was an explosion right next to me and a shower of sparks. I jumped and turned—just in time to see the jellyfish drifting through the window with a tentacle outstretched, over my shoulder. I dropped to the ground and rolled away, toward Isobel, who had already turned to see the horrible sight unfolding.

However, I needn't have worried.

The jellyfish's tentacle had missed me and, instead, struck the electrical panel. It was still connected to it, too, like it was glued there. Sparks were flying everywhere, and there was a loud crackling sound, like heavy static. The tentacle was smoking, and blue bolts of electricity were racing along it and swirling all over the jellyfish. Its color went from a glimmering green to a dirty brown. Within seconds, it fell to the floor in a wet, sloppy blob.

"Well, that takes care of one," Isobel said blankly.

Our attention turned to the blue jellyfish following Tony. It had cornered him at the end of the hall and had already begun lashing out with its tentacles. Tony, however, was quick with his garbage can lid, and he fended off the attacks like a ninja warrior. It wasn't long before the jellyfish collapsed in a heap on the carpet. There were hissing, popping sounds as the wet goop began to burn into the floor. Tony walked around the puddle of steaming gel and then ran to us.

"We did it!" he exclaimed. "We fried all of

the jellyfish attached to the neon lights!"

"But there are more around," Isobel said. "One just came through the broken window and almost got Shayleen."

"We'll still have to be careful," Tony said, "but maybe we can finally make it out of here."

I sure hoped he was right. I'd had enough of dealing with creepy jellyfish floating in the air. I wanted to get out of the amusement park. I wanted to see Mom and Dad and Lee.

"Let's head to the front of the building," Tony said. "From there, we should be able to see any more jellyfish, if they're around."

We ran through the hall, around the corner, and down the main hallway that led to the front of the building. In one of the offices, I spotted something I could use: a garbage can lid. I quickly snapped it up and ran after Tony and Isobel.

We raced to the front of the building. Before going out the door, we stopped at the window and looked outside.

"All clear, so far," Tony said. "I say we make a run for it. If everything goes well, we'll be out of the park in less than a minute."

"I'm all for that," I said, raising the garbage can lid I'd just snatched. "Especially since I've got another one of these."

Tony pushed open the door, and we cautiously stepped outside and into the open. We looked around. On all the rides, we saw the remains of what once had been jellyfish. In fact, there were so many piles of bubbling goo and so much smoke rising that it looked as if some of the rides were on fire. It was really freaky-looking.

"Follow us!" Tony said to me, and the three of us started running.

There are more jellyfish around, I thought. *We're going to be attacked at any moment. This isn't over by a long shot.*

However, as we raced through the park and saw no sign of any jellyfish, I became more hopeful. And when I saw the exit appear in the distance, I wanted to cheer out loud. There were police cars and fire trucks and flashing lights all over the place.

We ran even faster, knowing we'd finally made it. We were going to be okay. I could hear the police and firemen shouting to us, but I couldn't understand what they were saying. I thought they were urging us along, telling us to run faster. I had no idea they were trying to tell us there was a jellyfish attacking from behind us, until it was too late.

I was racing along the pavement, right behind Tony and Isobel. Not far ahead of us was the amusement park exit. It was swarmed by police cars and fire trucks. Several policemen and firemen were shouting to us. A few were pointing at us . . . or, I *thought* they were pointing at us. Actually, they were pointing *behind* us, and when I turned, I suddenly knew why.

There was a huge, red jellyfish only a few feet behind me!

I swung my arm around to raise my garbage

can lid, but the motion sent me off balance, and I fell.

The tumble knocked the wind from me. I was horrified. Time seemed to stop.

I was laying on my back, holding the garbage can lid over my chest and face, peering up over it at the jellyfish looming above. Its tentacles—black and yellow and glowing hot—dangled only inches from me. I knew that if it attacked, it would be nearly impossible for me to react in time.

Suddenly, there was a huge blast of water, and the jellyfish was gone. Water fell all over me, and I was instantly soaked from head to toe. I rolled to my side and stood, realizing what had happened: the firemen had used a fire hose on the jellyfish!

"Hurry!" one of them yelled to me. *"It's not going to stop him for good!"*

He wasn't going to have to tell me twice!

I ran and ran . . . and made it to the exit, where Tony, Isobel, the police, and firemen were waiting for me.

We were safe.

37

The police and firemen took us to our parents, who had been waiting on the other side of a barricade of vehicles. I sure was glad to see them again! Little Lee was happy, too, and when he saw me, he started jumping up and down. It was a happy ending, after all.

A policeman asked Tony, Isobel, and me all sorts of questions. Several other men and women were with him, and they all listened to us as we explained what we went through. We told them everything, but when we asked questions, they didn't have any answers. They had no idea where the strange jellyfish came from. They said that the jellyfish seemed to be attracted only to the neon lights of the amusement park. Whenever one had drifted close to the crowd, they'd been able to use the powerful water hoses from the fire trucks to knock it away and push it back.

Later that night, in our hotel room, the story about the jellyfish was all over the news. We even saw ourselves on television! Apparently, there had been a camera crew on the scene earlier in the day when we'd made our escape—we just didn't see them at the time.

They interviewed scientists and specialists, who offered their opinions. Most agreed that the jellyfish had, at one time, been 'normal' jellyfish, but something had happened to them to cause them to become charged with high amounts of energy. One of the scientists used the term 'nuclear,' which was the same word Tony had used to describe the jellyfish earlier that day. He said the creatures somehow 'fed' on the neon lights, using the energy as their own, and that the bright neon lights were probably what had attracted them to the amusement park in the first place.

And I couldn't help but wonder if what had happened to the jellyfish had anything to do with the strange, flying object we'd seen in the sky the night before. If so, why did it affect the jellyfish? Were there other creatures of the sea that had been affected, too?

But the bad news was the amusement park and water park were closed down while the investigation continued, and they had no idea how long it would be before they were re-opened. They thought all of the jellyfish had been destroyed, but they wanted to be sure.

However, considering all we'd been through that day, I was just glad to be alive. I was glad to be in our hotel room with Mom and Dad and Lee. Dad ordered pizza and had it delivered to our room, and we stayed indoors and watched the special news reports about the jellyfish and how they had attacked the park at Wildwood.

It wasn't long before I became tired. After all, it had been a long day, for sure. I gave Mom and Dad a hug and told them I was going to bed.

"I'll bet you're glad today's over," Mom said,

after she gave me a kiss on the cheek.

"You have no idea, Mom," I said. "I'll see you in the morning."

I walked into my room, changed into my nightgown, climbed into bed, and closed my eyes.

And that's when I heard a noise.

It was a soft, scraping sound, and it was very close. I opened my eyes and sat up, only to see a glowing purple tentacle coming out of the closet!

I opened my mouth and was about to scream, when I heard a giggle I'd recognize anywhere.

Lee.

I turned on the light by the bed, and the closet door opened. There was Lee, holding one of his glow sticks.

"You little stinker," I said with a laugh. "You scared me."

Lee stepped out of the closet and put his glow stick on the night stand, where it continued to glow brightly. He climbed onto the bed and was asleep before I was.

In the morning, the amusement park was still closed, but the Boardwalk was open. After breakfast, Mom, Dad, Lee, and I went for a walk. We overheard lots of conversations, and everyone seemed to be talking about the jellyfish. Lots of people were watching the skies curiously, as if they might see one of the strange creatures at any moment. I did my share of sky-gazing, too . . . but I never saw any more jellyfish.

All too soon, it was time to go home. It had been a fun vacation, even with the jellyfish. If my teacher at my new school asked us to write an essay about what we did on our summer vacation, I would have the best story in the class!

I said good-bye to Tony and Isobel, and I promised to write and keep in touch. They had become good friends in just a short time, and I really hoped I would see them again.

School started a few weeks later, and my new teacher did just what I thought: she asked us all to write about something we did on our summer vacation. I wrote all about what had happened at Wildwood, and I got an 'A.'

In October, Dad said he was taking a business trip back to Tennessee, where I grew up. He said he was going to drive and asked if I would like to come along. That would be great! I would get to see some of my old friends in Murfreesboro! Plus, our drive would take us through the Blue Ridge Mountains, which would be beautiful in the fall. I'd miss a few days of school, but I was getting good grades, and I could make up any tests.

We stopped to stretch our legs at a rest stop in West Virginia, and Dad made a couple of calls on his phone. I walked through the picnic area, where there was a boy about my age. He was walking his dog, a black Labrador.

"Cool dog," I said as the animal bounded up to me wagging his tail.

"That's Midnight," the boy said. "Don't worry. He doesn't bite. He's really friendly."

The dog just about tackled me, and he licked my hands playfully.

We talked while I petted Midnight. The boy said his name was Brandon Ellerbee, and he lived in Charleston, which is the state capital of West Virginia.

"We're on our way to visit my grandparents in Morgantown," he said. "We go there once or twice a year, and we always take Midnight. He loves to ride in the car. But we've got a flat tire. Dad is working on it right now."

I asked him about Charleston and what it was like. He said he's lived there all his life, not in the city, but on the outskirts. He said there's a lot of forest land where he lives and lots of hiking and biking trails.

"In fact," he said, "Charleston is where Dr. Wentmeyer has his laboratory."

"Who is Dr. Wentmeyer?" I asked.

"He's a scientist and an inventor," he replied. "He's pretty famous in West Virginia. In fact, it was because of him that my friend and I were attacked by dinosaurs."

"What?!?!" I exclaimed. What on earth was he talking about? "Real dinosaurs?!?!" I asked. "You're kidding, right?"

"No," he said, "I'm not kidding at all. In fact, I still get freaked out when I think about it."

I thought about what had happened on our vacation in New Jersey. *After that,* I thought, *I'd*

186

believe just about anything.

But dinosaurs? *Velociraptors?*

"Well, your dad is fixing a tire," I said, "and my dad is making some phone calls. We've got plenty of time. Tell me what happened."

Midnight laid down in the grass, and Brandon sat next to him.

"It happened only a few weeks ago," he began. I listened, spellbound, as he told me of the horrors he and his friend had faced with the wicked velociraptors of West Virginia . . . .

Next:

**#23: Wicked
Velociraptors
of
West Virginia**

**Continue on for
a FREE preview!**

1

"Ready?" Kara asked me.

"Go for it," I said, stooping forward and holding the baseball bat over my shoulder. "I'm going to knock this one into next week!"

It was Saturday, and my friend, Kara Haynes and I were practicing hitting a softball. Actually, *I* was the one working on my hitting. I think I'm a pretty good player, but the coach wanted me to work on my swings. He said I could be really good if I could hit the ball a little farther.

As for Kara? She didn't need to work on her

hitting or pitching. She's the only girl on the team, and for good reason. When it comes to softball, she can hit, run, and pitch. In fact, she's the team's starting pitcher. She's ten times better than any of the guys, and that makes some of them jealous.

Not me, though. I was just glad she was my friend, and she was willing to help me.

Midnight, my black Labrador, sat in the grass near the side of the road. We adopted him from a shelter last year, and he's the best dog in the whole world. He's really smart, and I include him as one of my best friends. Everywhere I go, Midnight goes. Except for school, of course.

Kara let the ball fly. As usual, her pitch was perfect. I swung as hard as I could . . . but the bat only skimmed the bottom of the ball, causing it to pop up into the air and arc down behind me. It rolled down the street.

"Midnight!" I shouted. Without saying anything more, Midnight leapt into action, chasing after the softball.

"You need to loosen up, Brandon," Kara called out. "You're too stiff. Let the bat flow with your body."

Easy for her to say.

The softball took a bounce over a curb and into the grass. Midnight snapped it up in his jaws while it was still rolling. He began trotted back to me, dropped the ball into my hand and sat.

"Good boy," I said, petting his head. "Go lay down." Midnight stood and walked to the side of the road, where he laid down again, ready to chase the ball again.

I paused for a moment to look around. Here, near the end of our block, there weren't very many houses. That's why it was a good place to practice hitting: there wasn't much danger of hitting anything or anyone. Sure, it would be a lot better if we could practice at the softball field, but the closest one was ten miles away. Kara lived on the same block I did, so it was a lot easier and more convenient to hike to the end of the block and practice.

Kara was still standing in the middle of the road with her right hand on her hips. Her left hand, covered by a worn, leather softball glove, hung loose at her side. Her glossy black hair shined in the late morning sun, and she was squinting as she watched me.

"Did you hear what I said?" she asked.

"Yeah," I replied. "You said I need to loosen up."

"You can still swing hard," she said, "just try not to be so tense. And be sure to follow through with your swing." She grasped an invisible bat and made a slow swing.

"Let's try again," I said, tossing the ball to her. She snapped it out of the air with her glove.

"You'll get it," she said, and I was glad for her encouragement. "Just keep your eyes focused on the ball, and stay loose."

I pulled the bat over my right shoulder and spread my feet apart.

"Loosen up your shoulders," Kara said. "You need to be comfortable."

Now that Kara mentioned it, I noticed my shoulder muscles were really tight. I relaxed a little, and took a deep breath.

"That's it," Kara said, winding up. "Here it comes."

And here it goes, I thought. *I'm going to really nail this one.*

She threw the softball, and when it was right in the perfect zone, I swung. The bat connected with a solid *thwack!* and the softball went flying.

"That's the way!" Kara shouted as the softball soared high over her head. I don't think I'd ever hit a ball so hard or so high. It sailed up, over the tree tops, and vanished.

"Holy crow!" I shouted. "That's a home run if I ever saw one!"

My elation and excitement, however, was short lived. Seconds later, we heard the distant, distinct sound of shattering glass. Midnight flinched and let out a single, startled bark.

I dropped the bat, and it clunked to the pavement.

Oh, no, I thought. *This isn't just bad. This is terrible. A disaster.*

You see, it was bad enough I'd broken a window . . . but what made matters worse was the fact that the only home in that direction belonged to none other than Dr. Joseph Wentmeyer.

And everyone knew that not only was Dr. Wentmeyer a mean person, he was also as crazy as a loon.

I had broken his window, and I would have to face him. I was scared to even get *close* to his house, let alone have to speak with him.

Now, however, as I look back, facing Dr. Wentmeyer wasn't the worst part. Oh, it was bad, all right. You see, if I hadn't broken the window, I wouldn't have to face Dr. Wentmeyer . . . and I wouldn't have had to face the velociraptors.

Breaking a window was bad enough.

Breaking Dr. Wentmeyer's window made it much worse. Sure, it was an accident. I never imagined I would have been able to hit the ball hard enough to reach his house. His home wasn't even visible from where we were, because there was a line of thick trees that grew all around it. It was as if they were planted there on purpose, to hide the house from the outside world.

"Uh-oh," Kara said. "That's not good."

"You can say that again," I said. I felt like I

wanted to crawl into a hole. Once, I accidentally broke a window in our house. Dad and Mom were mad, but it had been an accident, and I didn't get into too much trouble.

Breaking someone else's window, however, was a different story.

"I've got to tell Dr. Wentmeyer that I was the one who broke his window," I said. I picked up the bat. "Come on, Midnight."

Midnight got to his feet, shook, and trotted up to me.

"I'll go with you," Kara said. "After all: it's my fault, too. If I wasn't such a good pitcher, you would never have been able to hit the ball as hard as you did."

I smiled. Kara wasn't bragging, she was only being funny. Besides: she really was a great pitcher.

We walked down the street, and I must say I wasn't in any hurry. I wasn't looking forward to confronting Dr. Wentmeyer. I'd never spoken to him before in my life, and the only things I knew about him were what my friends and classmates had told me.

At his driveway, we stopped. His three-story house loomed up, and it seemed to become part of the sky and trees. A black iron gate was open, but the fence continued around the property to keep people out. There were signs posted that read 'KEEP OUT!' and 'NO TRESPASSING.'

"Looks like Dr. Wentmeyer is a really friendly guy," Kara said.

"Yeah," I said. "And he's going to be even friendlier when he finds out I broke one of his windows."

"I don't see anything broken," Kara said. "Maybe you didn't break a window."

"Oh, I'm sure it was a window," I said. "But the angle the ball would have dropped from is over there." I pointed. "It probably hit a window on the other side of his house. Come on."

"But his signs say he doesn't want anyone trespassing," Kara said.

"Yeah, but this is different," I said. "We're not trespassing, we're coming to tell him that we broke one of his windows. It would be worse just to leave and not say anything about it."

I started up the driveway with Midnight at

my side. Kara followed.

"It sure looks like a lonely place," Kara said. "It doesn't look like he's home."

We walked up the driveway and stepped up onto the porch. The front door was solid wood, with a brass doorknob and a brass knocker. I reached out and rapped several times. We listened for any sounds from within the house, but there were none.

I rapped several more times.

Still, Dr. Wentmeyer didn't come to the door.

"He's probably not home," Kara said.

"Let's walk around to the other side of the house," I said as I stepped off the porch. "Let's see if we can find the broken window. If we have to, we can leave Dr. Wentmeyer a note."

We strode around to the other side of the house. Sure enough, we found a broken window. It was on the first floor, and there was a distinct hole in the glass where the softball had hit. Pieces of the window had broken out, and a few of them had fallen to the grass.

"Sit, Midnight," I said, and he obeyed

immediately.

I walked up to the window, mindful of the glass at my feet.

"I think the ball must have went into the house," I said. "I don't see it anywhere."

There were no curtains on the window, and I decided to peer inside to see if I could see my softball. I knew I shouldn't because it was like spying or something. But I had to know.

I hope I didn't break anything inside, I thought. *A broken window is bad enough.*

I stood on my tiptoes and looked inside.

I didn't see my softball . . . but what I *did* see made me gasp.

"Kara!" I exclaimed. *"Come here! You've got to see this!"*

ABOUT THE AUTHOR

Johnathan Rand is the author of more than 50 books, with well over 2 million copies in print. Series include **AMERICAN CHILLERS, MICHIGAN CHILLERS, FREDDIE FERNORTNER, FEARLESS FIRST GRADER**, and **THE ADVENTURE CLUB.** He's also co-authored a novel for teens (with Christopher Knight) entitled **PANDEMIA.** When not traveling, Rand lives in northern Michigan with his wife and two dogs. He is also the only author in the world to have a store that sells only his works: **CHILLERMANIA!** is located in Indian River, Michigan. Johnathan Rand is not always at the store, but he has been known to drop by frequently. Find out more at:

www.americanchillers.com

FUN FACTS ABOUT NEW JERSEY

State Capital: Trenton

Largest City: Newark

Statehood: December 18th, 1787

State Nickname: The Garden State

State Colors: Buff and Blue

State Insect: Honeybee

State Fish: Brook Trout

State Animal: Horse

State Bird: Eastern Goldfinch

State Flower: Violet

State Tree: Northern Red Oak

State Dinosaur: Hadrosaurus Foulkii

FAMOUS PEOPLE FROM NEW JERSEY

Norman Mailer - Novelist

Philip Roth - Novelist

Richard Nixon - President

Frank Sinatra - Singer and Actor

Bruce Springsteen - Musician

Bud Abbot - Comedian

Lou Costello - Comedian

Jon Bon Jovi - Musician

Sarah Vaughan - Singer

Jerry Lewis - Comedian

Allen Ginsberg - Poet

Count Basie - Band Leader

among many, many more!

Join the official

AMERICAN CHILLERS

FAN CLUB!

Visit www.americanchillers.com for details!

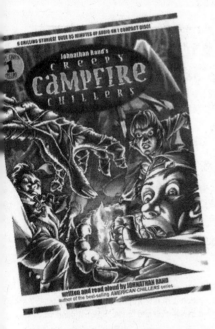

Johnathan Rand travels internationally for school visits and book signings! For booking information, call:

1 (231) 238-0338!

www.americanchillers.com

All AudioCraft books are proudly printed, bound, and manufactured in the United States of America, utilizing American resources, labor, and materials.

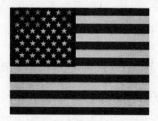

USA